SLEEP ALONE

A novella by
J.A.W. McCARTHY

Praise for *SLEEP ALONE*

"A sensual, synesthetic tour through the dive bars of the Pacific Northwest with a most unusual band, *SLEEP ALONE* grapples with ethical questions about responsibility and care even as it revels in sex, drugs, and body horror. I couldn't look away."—Christi Nogle, author of *BEULAH*

"McCarthy's all grunge, sex, and distortion in her latest offering *Sleep Alone*. You feel the bass reverberate through your bones, smell the sweat and sensuality of the downtown club buzzing with anticipation, and there—the eyes of someone, or something, coaxing you in as the van door slides open, but by then it's too late."—Scott J. Moses, author of *Our Own Unique Affliction*

"This queer rock 'n' roll road trip from Hell is an endlessly inventive exploration of desire, control, and companionship. Sleep Alone had me cheering for an encore."—Eric Raglin, author of *Extinction Hymns*

"*Sleep Alone* is a feral howl of longing for found family, a gory road trip, a sensual rock & roll adventure through human and inhuman hungers. McCarthy's language satisfies like a gorgeous and intoxicating feast. While the book drips with insatiable desire, it also asks us in the most heartfelt way to take responsibility for our love in its many forms."—Joe Koch, author of *The Wingspan of Severed Hands*

for Matt, Laika, and the real Cillian

1.

This is how it is when you're a merch girl:

The club manager or promoter comes up to you while you're trying to set up the merch table, calls you "sweetheart" or "ma'am," and tells you to go wait with the other groupies.

You can't hear the customer because it's so damn loud and maybe you've suffered some hearing loss, but you don't want them to know that because they're all younger than you and they already think you're old.

You keep toilet paper and baby wipes in your purse, always.

The bouncer won't let you in the green room with the band because he thinks you're a fan, but not a hot enough one.

The guitarist buys you drinks every night because you fucked him once, and that's his way of saying he'd like to do it again.

Both before and after your band plays, you get to watch them move through the crowd, catching eyes and feeding while you're stuck behind the merch table, starving.

They eat and eat and eat, and you're so hungry. You're hungry all the time.

Does it matter what kind of music they play? Mostly dirty rock, a little metal, sometimes psychobilly when the bassist gets his way. I like it because it's an outlet, something to feel other than the hunger.

The band is a working band, occupying a broad, liminal space between being nobodies to most and rock stars to some. They're recognized enough to headline in the smaller towns and open for bigger acts in the cities. Their demands—pizza, beer, clean towels, ranch dressing on the party platter—are just enough to show they know what they're worth, but not so much that they can't be fulfilled by any backwoods dive. Their website has plenty of photos and song clips, though anything beyond first names was scrubbed long ago. Our return address is a PO box in southern California or New Jersey, depending on which end of the country we're in when the occasional t-shirt or bootleg order comes in. What few belongings we don't take with us reside in a storage space outside of L.A. We rent by-the-hour rehearsal spaces whenever inspiration or boredom strikes. Even in the tiny venues a true fan or two will show up, but not so many that we can't feed and slip out unnoticed. We'll sell enough merch to get us to the next town, the next place where we can make a little money and eat again.

Tonight, it's somewhere north of Portland and south of Seattle. The cities are spaced farther apart in the northwest, so you have to hit every little dive with the promise of warm bodies if you want to make any money. What no one tells you is you can make more money in these little towns. In the big cities there's too much competition, too many choices, so it's not worth taking a chance on a band you've maybe only vaguely heard of. In the little towns people come out because there's nothing else to do and the band's playing in their local watering hole anyway.

At the end of the first band's set, Jack brings me a gin and tonic. Our band goes on next, and he's got that frazzled look, all wavering lines under his black t-shirt and faded black jeans. His fingers will be vibrating against his guitar if he doesn't shake it off now.

"How's it going, Ronnie? Any sales so far?"

The question used to be "Did you eat yet?", but he knows damn well all I ever get to eat before a show is whatever shitty pizza satisfies the band's rider. He'll pretend he waits for me, but the truth is he isn't able to eat until after they play. Still, it's cute that after all these years he still gets nervous before a show, that his stomach's a rollercoaster of bile and knots until after he steps off the stage.

"Some shirts, a little over $200—We're getting low on larges again," I tell him. "You know we always sell the albums after you guys play."

Jack smiles. If we sell enough shirts and albums we can get a second room at the motel down the road, so he won't have to sleep in the van with the singer, who snores.

"What do you think of this town?"

He asks me this at least four times in every state, a glint of hope in his hazel eyes, and I always answer the same:

"It's like any other."

He thinks we—me, him, the band—should settle somewhere soon. Sylvy, the drummer, even jokes that we're getting old, that soon it will be too late for kids, for family. The boys know that with what we do—with the mistakes we've made—we have to keep moving, and that is usually all I need to say.

What they don't know, what I can't bring myself to tell them, is that they are not fully like me. I am one in ten million, and my boys are even rarer. Succubi like them shouldn't exist, but I didn't care about rules and reasons when I made them. Only those born a succubus can create, and what I've created is an abomination—a selfish itch selfishly scratched—that means even if we could lay our heads in the same place every night, I will always sleep alone.

By the time the band takes the stage, everyone is sated except for Jack. You can tell who's had what and how much, and even what the show's going to be like tonight.

Cillian, the singer, eats the most. You could say it's tied to frontman ego and all that, but I think he'd be just as greedy if he were a suburban high school principal. From my vantage point to the left of the stage, I see two girls— late teens or early twenties; they're so small it's hard to tell—near the back, clinging to each other as they sway with, then against, the music. To everyone else they look drunk, maybe a little too loose and jelly from the molly, and soon a bouncer will scoop them up and to the side when the crowd starts sweeping over them. The one with the black hair is flushed, cheeks red as the lipstick smeared outside the lines of her mouth because that's how Cillian prefers to do it, through the mouth. Her friend, the blonde, has perfect makeup, razor-sharp purple lips and eyeliner. The back of her skirt is tucked into her underwear, and she's giggling so hard she falls to her knees. I wonder what was so special that Cillian got out of her, where he took her since he usually doesn't like the bother of seeking privacy.

There's an older guy slumped over his beer at the bar. He's wearing one of our old tour shirts from ten years ago. In profile his face is all dark pools and bronze planes, except his cheeks are puffed out with a mouthful of what is likely fresh vomit. He's Drew's—the bass player—pre-show snack. We usually don't go after the old fans, the true fans, the ones who know every line and every air guitar chord, but now and then one of the boys will take just a little, when the road's been too long and they're starting to forget.

The woman sitting on the vodka-cranberry-sticky floor near the exit is Sylvy's. She's dazed, head down, a strobing outline as her friend rubs her back in the glow of her phone's screen. Her arms are flopped slack at her sides, the ropes of her once impressive biceps and triceps loose and sloppy and pooling together. I could've guessed our drummer would choose her after he was complaining about how sore his arms were last night.

Two songs in and Cillian grows more animated, more reckless, as the crowd screams and hoists their drinks and sings along. He leans as horizontal as his mic stand, only one foot keeping him on the ground. His eyes are crazed, and his shaggy blue-black hair seems to rise into little spikes all over his head as if he's a cartoon kid with his finger in a light socket. Electricity runs in blue lines up the sides of his neck and along his strained jaw, mouth stretched so wide I realize I've never seen all his teeth before and they are so white and so wet. They were already yellowing with age when I put my mouth on his all those years ago. Now he's bright and ageless, as slick as an icon.

My attention is pulled from the stage when I see a guy pour out of the bar's bathroom on his hands and knees. With his sinewy arms poking out of a too-big t-shirt, he could be a kid who brown-bagged it and snuck in or a thirty-something drained almost dry. What's left of his blue lines are broken, hissing, and spitting sparks off his trembling frame. He lifts a hand towards the stage, then goes face down when his other arm gives out.

Fucking Cillian. When someone notices this kid and calls an ambulance, we all better hope he's too empty to remember what Cillian did to him.

I sell two shirts, a bunch of patches, and six copies of the band's last album before I look at the bar bathroom again and see that the kid is gone. The two bouncers are at their posts at the front of the stage. The two girls Cillian had earlier are now sitting down on either side of a pillar by the bar, arms linked and eyes closed. I don't see the woman with the arms or her friend anywhere. Every time someone opens one of the exit doors I expect to see the flash of blue and white lights, but there are none.

Jack smiles at me. He's blind from the stage lights, but he knows where I am and he always seems to know when things are about to go wrong.

2.

Nothing goes wrong because though I can't control this band, I can control myself.

While the band loads out, I pack up what's left of the merch. Once the house lights went up most of the audience left, but I see one guy at the bar unabashedly staring at me over the top of his Rainier bottle. He's not as young as I would prefer. Right now, under the low lights of the club and the streetlights outside, I look passable, but I'll have to eat again in the morning if I want to leave the motel room during the day. But he'll be easy. And the weary bartenders look like they'll be happy to deliver him to me gift wrapped if I get him out of their hair for the night.

I pretend I don't notice as he approaches me. I pretend to demure under his drunk, watery eyes outlining my body every time I bend down.

"Need some help?" he asks once I've got the banner rolled up and packed in the last box. He follows limply behind me as I shove the cash in my jeans and carry the boxes to the stage.

The guy doesn't know it, but what he likes about me is that I don't have a lot of time. I let him push me up against the wall by the bathrooms, guiding his sloppy hands but letting him think he's kissing me, he's the one in control. Across the small club, Sylvy smirks and arches an eyebrow at me as he collects his cymbal stands. I close my eyes and try to get my mouth open under the man's lips, gasping for a little taste in the moments when his lips roam to the wrong places. His mouth, his skin, tastes like the hopelessness I felt growing up: skunk weed cottonmouth, stale saltines stuck in the crevices of molars, salt and grease on a fast food bag. The good stuff is deeper down, but he's not letting me in yet. I calculate how long I have until the band is ready to leave, how long it will take Jack to account for his cords then choose one of the drunks still lingering in the parking lot so he can finally eat. When I open my eyes again, I see a woman standing next to the now-empty stage, staring right at me.

Her.

How had I not noticed her before? Short hair shining blue-black under the cold fluorescents with bangs like long canines slipping down her forehead. Black muscle shirt over second-skin moto jeans. Pointy boots with silver tips that look like they've rebuked a brazen hand or two. Expression unreadable, gaze unshakeable. Is this where she usually drinks? Did she come at the end of the night so she wouldn't have to pay the cover? She stares at me with eyes so dark I can feel the magnets behind them, an open void to a potent core that is at once intoxicating and familiar.

I slide my hand down inside the guy's pants, take his tongue in my mouth and keep my eyes on *her* as she continues to stare in the same calm, set manner. He moves so that he's blocking my view, so I push his head aside. The woman smiles, then turns towards the back exit to the parking lot.

When the house lights come all the way on, it's time to go outside.

As we climb into the back seat of the guy's car—Paul? Saul? He didn't even ask my name, so why should I remember his?—I scan the now mostly empty parking lot and the streets beyond, but I don't see the woman anywhere. Paul/Saul undoes his fly and pulls me onto his lap while I've still got one leg in my jeans. He doesn't seem to mind that I'm more interested in wiping away the condensation from the rear window so I can look out. Now it's just the band's van left in the load zone, and a few cars that probably belong to the club's staff parked at the far end of the lot. Cillian and Sylvy meander along the side of the van in the cold while Drew is curled in the backseat, arms crossed over his stomach when he isn't fiddling with the hem of his t-shirt. I wonder where Jack is eating. I wonder if he found the woman with the blue-black hair first, if she was standing by the stage, waiting for him.

The girls, the older fan, the woman with the arms, and the kid on his knees are all likely tucked safely in the back of ride shares, headed for the comfort of their own beds. In the morning they won't remember much; there will be just a headache and the muddy throb of what they think is the music still in their veins to mark what happened the night before. They had a good time, like any other night, and nothing went wrong.

Paul/Saul doesn't have anything special that I want, so when I open up that part of myself deep inside my core— what makes me a succubus, the tunnel that is never satisfied—I pull into my body a little energy, a little memory, just enough to get me through and remove whatever he might retain of this night. I won't take enough to kill him, not if I don't have to. Feeding and fucking aren't the same, but they're both a means to an end, and men especially leave themselves most open when you're fucking them.

So, Paul/Saul is happy, making little grunts as he wets the hollow of my throat, thinking he's the only one getting what he wants. I'm out of his car before he even has his pants buttoned up.

Jack joins me and the rest of the guys minutes later, his lips swollen and splotchy. Our movements are heavy as we climb into the van.

At the motel, we get a second room. Drew and Cillian stay in the old room. Jack and Sylvy share a bed in the new room. I get the other bed to myself. I'm tired, but I can't fall asleep because I can't stop thinking about that woman. *Her*. I'm still so hungry.

3.

The whole place smells sour and musty, like a PBR burp. No matter how many bodies are packed in here tonight, stirring up clouds of sugary vanilla perfume and aqua-something body spray, it's not enough to cover up the stench.

We're somewhere north of Seattle and south of Bellingham. Two shows—one south and one in Tacoma—last night, and the whole band is exhausted, though Cillian complains the loudest. During the opening band's set, I catch him eyeing the guy who comes to my table. The guy is young, maybe late twenties, wearing a shirt from the last tour, the one with the epically-quiff-ed Frankenstein monster that Sylvy drew. He flips through the vinyl I've fanned out, then moves on to the display shirts, grinning and humming to himself the whole time.

"No new shirts for this tour?" he asks, the sharp lines of his grey lipstick making exaggerated shapes. His head bobs to the music, and when he jerks his shoulders side to side a wave of what smells like rum and Coke sails out of his plastic cup.

"Sorry," I say.

"Aw man, that's too bad. It's my birthday, and I get a shirt every time I see you guys."

Before I can get a "happy birthday" out, the guy is surrounded by half the occupants of the bar. They're patting him on the back, hugging him, bringing him beers and cocktails in plastic cups, more than he can carry. They jump up and down with him, screaming, spinning, twirling him as their enthusiastic ribbon on a maypole. Six people buy him pins and patches, and a bootleg that he doesn't already have. After the birthday guy's friends sweep him away, I see Jack across the room giving me a thumbs up. Cillian is still staring at the guy, the singer's laser focus a stark contrast to the rest of his body slumped against the bar.

Jack brings me another G&T, but I lose track of the rest of the band before they hit the stage. While the guy selling merch for the other band is busy now, I sit back, my table empty as my band's fans gather around the stage. It's a good turnout for a Wednesday night, enough that we'll be able to pay for two motel rooms again and a breakfast that doesn't come from a vending machine tomorrow morning.

The band ascends the stage to applause and cheering. Cillian positively glows; if only he could feed on adoration alone. They dive right into the music, no intros necessary in this town, not when beers are held aloft and everyone knows every word. I watch and drink my G&T too fast. I don't get up until they start playing my favorite song.

My song.

The heavy thump of the bass carries me, guides my head and my hips even though I prefer it when Drew slaps his standup. I sway in front of my merch table, following Jack's fingers on the guitar, nodding my head to the thrash of Sylvy's drums. Cillian is a new man tonight: he kicks over the mic stand, paces the stage in huge strides, leans down into the audience so they can sing with him. Everyone knows this song too, and it makes me swell with pride. The band wrote this song right after we met, after I made them. They play it every set, their nightly tithe to me, a little thank you. When strangers sing along, I don't regret anything.

Who doesn't get a little wild when they look at the moon?
Just watch out boy, because tonight the monster isn't you…

My whole body is throbbing with the bass, kicked in the ribs by the snare. The energy of every person in the horror-movie red room shoots up the soles of my boots. I think of the birthday guy jumping around with his friends, but I don't see him in the audience. I'm scanning the bar when I see *her*.

Leather jacket tonight, but the same moto jeans and pointy boots that I don't want to get in the way of. Did she come to the shows last night? No, I wouldn't have missed her, no fucking way. What is she doing here? She would've had to drive three hours from that southern Washington show, and she doesn't strike me as one of the band's biggest fans. But she's watching the band, and though her mouth is slouched in a serious line, she's nodding her head and holding her drink high every time the crowd cheers.

If you're lucky, she'll give as good as she takes…
Just remember that you've always been hers to make…

All too aware of how stupid I look, I fumble my way behind the merch table. I pray for someone to come up and buy something, but I don't want to take my eyes off *her* either. Then she turns towards me, hair still glowing blue-black even in this venue's red light, and before I can look away, she smiles. Same unshakeable gaze, but this time I can read her.

Her name is Helene.

She asks me my name right away, and in her mouth the sound of my O and Ns is warm cream rolling off her tongue. She says "Ronnie, I like your necklace", "Ronnie, do you always tour with the band?", "What are you drinking, Ronnie?", and I'm at once melting and wondering what she thinks she can get from me.

Helene buys us G&Ts, and we take them back to the merch table. We nod along to the headlining band, but I notice she is watching the audience, same as me. There's a woman staggering through the crowd, hands out and grasping at shoulders, cheeks puffed as if she is about to vomit. Dark, wavy hair, big eyes, round face. She looks like Jack's type. She looks like me. Drew and Sylvy are sitting at the bar, still glistening with sweat under the low lights. Jack's getting his beer and his body sloshed around in the pit. I don't see Cillian anywhere.

"So, where are you from?" Helene asks. *You*, not *you guys*.

I give her my usual answer: "All over." When I return the question, she says the exact same thing.

We go back and forth like this, deflecting, asking the things you're supposed to ask, saying the things you're supposed to say, the pointless prologue to what we both came here for. I focus on her lips making shapes, the glint of her teeth peeking out from behind those wet, pink slopes. She's smooth lines sizzling under leather, a pulse that laps at my toes then up through the soles of my boots just like my favorite song. I can hardly hear what she's saying, but I know what I want from her—what she wants from me—in the little movements of her body as she talks.

I am so hungry.

We abandon the merch table for the narrow gravel and grass alley behind the building. "Fresh air," she says, but

14

neither of us needs the suggestion. It's cold, so we huddle close, close enough for my mouth to find hers.

I always start with a kiss. Unlike Cillian, I don't prefer the mouth—there are more direct ways to get what I need—but you've got to start somewhere. And unlike with so many of the others, I want to kiss Helene. I want to taste every part of her before I take it all.

She tastes the way animals' ears smell: rich, oily, tangy, alive. The gin on her lips turns mineral-y, meaty against my own. As we kiss, I taste melted butter, the hot breath of shower steam, soft smooth skin stretched tight over muscle, clean sheets up to my chin on a Sunday morning. Contentment. Then, under that, my tongue finds that animal flavor again, the feral tang of restlessness. Hunger.

Her skin is as familiar as the inside of my own mouth.

Inside the club the music slows to a throb and the cheers grow louder, a crescendo that tells me that the last song is about to be played and soon dozens of bodies will spill out the door just a few feet away from Helene and me. We move faster, fingers fumbling over layers of shirts and belts and things that should be obedient beneath our touch. I get one more long, lingering taste of her, then I open up that part of myself deep inside my core, unclenching the tunnel that creates a direct route to my mouth, and I start to pull everything I can take from her *up, up, up* through her body and into mine.

Except I can't get much—it's like she keeps her energy locked behind a wall, as if she knows what I'm trying to do. All I can pull into my mouth is a flash of me dancing in front of the merch table, crystal-clear in an otherwise distorted droplet of her memory that sizzles to vapor when it hits my tongue. Her lips still pressed to mine, she takes a deep breath and suddenly the tunnel goes the other way, and I feel my whole body start to turn inside out, all of the strength anchored deep in my core rising up my stomach, my chest, my throat—

We break away from each other at the same time. Hands braced on thighs, we're both doubled-over, trembling, struggling to draw in air that's turned to ice somewhere between the water and the mountains. We stare at each other; she's smiling. Helene's eyes are wide and shiny, endless black pupils that reflect my own stunned expression.

She backs into the dumpster, hard enough to jostle the opposite end of it out from against the building's brick exterior. We both jump. A head and torso in a t-shirt from our last tour flops out from behind, a loose arm scattering gravel against my boots.

The body looks like that of an old man: brittle, wizened, the crepe-y skin of his once fleshy arm now vacuum-sealed over chicken wing bones. But he's not an old man, and I recognize him right away: It's the birthday guy, grey lipstick smeared all around the outside of his mouth.

4.

Everyone's pissed.

Jack is mad at me because I left the merch table unattended, and someone took the $150 we made tonight. Sylvy's mad because we have to skip the two shows we had booked outside of Vancouver. Drew's mad because he's got another one of his stomachaches. Cillian is mad because we're heading east instead. And everyone's mad at Cillian because he went too far.

At least they've eaten. Yes, Helene and I could feed on each other, walk that tightrope of giving a little, taking a little, but there's a reason why our kind doesn't make that a habit. I have before, in times of desperation, when I first made the band and they were too young and too wild to feed themselves, to control themselves, but it left me vulnerable when my trust is not that deep.

The boys don't know Helene is like us. They eye her waiting for me in her car, but they seem more irritated than threatened. They think I'm going to empty her, leave her dazed and worn in the parking lot or on the side of the road, no memory of this night, but not so disoriented that she thinks someone slipped something in her drink. A quick snack. Except there's a dead body.

This isn't the first time we've split town in the middle of the night, no time to piss or grab the few things we left in the motel room. I ride with Helene in her car, following close behind the van. I can't stop sneaking glances at her, wondering why she would choose to run off with us—with *me*. This isn't some all-consuming love at first sight, despite the way my stomach tumbles every time she meets my gaze. It's lust. It's hunger. And for her, probably

17

boredom too. I tasted all those comforts on her lips: shower steam, clean sheets, that soft skin over taut muscle; whatever she has at home is as easy as it is unsatisfying.

Perhaps Helene is running from something, though I don't dare ask as if even acknowledging the possibility might send her skittering from my outstretched hand like a feral cat. She says she was heading east anyway—a little road trip—and though I don't believe her, I'm not worried that she wants anything from me or the band because she knows we're all the same. None of us are worth the fight.

Still, we are so hungry.

Four hours later, in a town buried deep in the Cascades, we stop at a motel for the night. We're a memorable bunch, but Cillian spins a good story about how we're headed west to Seattle to play a festival, and that's enough for the curious innkeeper. No one says anything about Helene because we're all still mad. I can guess what Jack's thinking as he watches us, though, and I know he sees my hunger no matter how far I push it down, no matter how much more he is willing to give me.

I can admit this now: I did it all wrong.

I went to a show and fell in love with the music. I've fallen in love before, of course, heard a song, a melody, a voice that stood out from all of the others and turned my body electric, charged my heart and made it beat same as the drums, made me inhale with the guitar and exhale with the bass, kept my mouth open and my tongue leaning hard against every word. Not just an ear worm, but something that fills my head and my chest enough to—however momentarily—obliterate the ache, the hunger. I've collected bootlegs and B-sides, made sure to see this or that favorite band every time they came to my town. It's a love most people know.

They were different, though, this band. I was hungry and restless, and I walked into a bar to satiate those ever-present needs. I didn't know who they were, but there they were: Cillian laying into the mic, growling and spitting and crooning words that lost all meaning in that miasma of sound; Jack, back arched and fingers moving with unexpected grace as he tore into his guitar; Drew slapping and abusing his stand-up bass in ways I never knew were possible; Sylvy in a tornado of black hair and perspiration behind the drums as he brought the whole thing down. They were more alive than anyone I'd seen in a long time. They were kind of terrible.

This was six years ago, though, but it wasn't like I could discern much about musical talent at that time. I was the kid who got dropped by her piano teacher, the kid who got put in the back of the choir and told to just mouth the words, the kid who was given the triangle to play in the fourth grade band. Growing up, learning what I was, I needed an outlet, something that didn't keep me in the shadows like my mother wanted. It didn't matter that my fingers fumbled over strings and keys and I couldn't carry a tune. Those musicians I admired travelled the world. They were as hungry and restless as I was, and they had found the perfect way to feed their needs.

But that night, seeing that band—*my* band—didn't calm me, didn't satiate me as I'd expected and experienced before. Instead, they charged my hunger. I wanted to rip everyone in that bar apart, drain them all, carry all their memories of this night, their adrenaline and their lust in my gut and between my legs. I wanted to fight. I wanted to fuck.

That's how this band was different.

So I got swept up. I saw the way people looked at the band, the rapt faces even if it was only a few. Though the air was weighted down with B.O. and body spray, it sizzled. I nearly drained a drunk woman of all her motor functions in the bathroom, only stopping when someone kicked in the stall door. After the show, I got friendly with the band in the alley as they were loading out. They invited me back to their motel. Then, instead of draining them and taking all they had, as I had intended, something occurred to me: we could be like this forever. So, that night, after the boys slipped into a booze-lulled sleep, I climbed onto each one of them and had a little taste of everything they had to offer. To them, it was just sex with a particularly hospitable fan, so they willingly gave me what I needed, and I made room in their bodies to accept what I would give. I took and took, *up up up* right to the brink of realization, to their own mortality. Then, as their eyes grew hard and dark as rabbits' as the pleasure spiked to panic, I did something I'd never done before: I opened up my tunnel, turned it inside out and pushed parts of myself I'd never shared into their supine, hungry bodies. I didn't know if it was going to work—I didn't know what I was doing; my mother had left me nothing beyond instinct—but the morning proved me right. They were like me. It seemed failsafe at the time, knowing that because they were not born succubi, they couldn't make any of their own.

"I knew they were yours," Helene says after I tell her all this.

I don't know why I told her any of it; it's a story that belongs to me and the band, not a transient moment of connection in a transient stretch of night. There's something about the way Helene listens, the way she watches me, her soft focus somehow both welcoming and reserved. Like she knows that she doesn't need to open me up; she's more satisfied by the surprise of what will come out when I do it on my own.

She scoots to the edge of the bed, finds her t-shirt on the floor, and pulls it on over her head. Her hair smooths back down with the motion, unmarred black lacquer poured into shape as if nothing happened between us. "That night, when I first saw you, I knew," she says. "Your scent's all over them."

I think of the boys in the next room, Jack and Drew in one bed and Cillian and Sylvy in the other, all curled on their sides, backs to each other and limbs stretched for dominance. Bellies full, no empty spaces. They had each other long before me, but I'm the one who curls around them and keeps them in a knot so tight that I become frayed when they're hungry, when they're restless, when they stray.

"I don't know if I didn't take enough from them, or if I'm just a lost cause," I say, watching black fabric drape Helene's hips as she rises from the bed. Our shirts are almost the same; I wish I had thought to dress first, to grab hers and put it on so her scent can be all over me after she leaves. "I've never had any musical talent. I can't carry a tune." I force a laugh because she's looking at me, immutable, and I have to fill all the space she's giving me. "So I'm the merch girl."

"If they've done things like this before—things that put you in danger—why do you stay with them? You could travel on your own. You don't need them."

"I made them."

"Is a parent responsible for their child once they're an adult? When does it stop? You made them, but they don't belong to you, and you don't belong to them. They're not your purpose, Ronnie," Helene says, looking at me over her shoulder. I can see my last kiss on her, a mark on her jawline still glistening with my saliva. "How many years has it been? They were only your responsibility at first. What you've done…it doesn't have to own you."

There were plenty of nights when Cillian was greedy, and Drew was sloppy, and Sylvy thought he could be quick behind the drum riser before the lights came up. And every one of those nights I considered draining them and leaving their empty husks in the motel room for the housekeeper to find—I could do what they can if I did it right this time, if I took everything—but there are still cities left, still other places we haven't been. It's true that I acted rashly, that I wanted to live out a fantasy of belonging, of family. Maybe I was afraid to end it. Maybe I was afraid to do it alone. Maybe I'm too afraid to do what my kind are meant to do and take it all.

Again, the urge to tell Helene all this is sudden and strong, but I stop myself. Though there was a moment when she opened up enough for me to take what I needed from her, I didn't—not even a taste—and I don't want to do that anymore, not to people I care about, not to her. I don't want to have to take her memory of this night.

"If you knew what I was when you first saw me, why did you go out to the alley with me?" I ask.

Helene raises an eyebrow. "Well, I wasn't sure. I mean, I was pretty sure, but I had to find out," she says, lips pressing into a wicked little grin.

I want to kiss her. The taste of her is already fading in my mouth. "So, you were going to drain me?"

"*You* were going to drain *me*."

"Not drain. Just a little. Enough to survive." I'm buoyed by that smile that lingers, the sharp points of her lips and eyes that lift her face and hold the door wide open for me. "And I wanted you. I wanted to fuck you," I add.

"Same here."

Helene does a little twirl, and it surprises me; her self-assuredness makes her seem somehow older than me, though I'm not that young myself. In a dark club, in our thick eyeliner and black t-shirts, we can pass for twenty-somethings, we can blend in because our stance shows we belong. In the daytime, when I'm alone and I haven't eaten, my age becomes clearer, makes me vulnerable. One night with Helene, though—even now with the orange glow of this motel room highlighting the mascara streaks filling the lines under my eyes, making years of baggage even darker, even heavier—I feel young and naive. I want her to show me everything before she disappears, before she moves on to someone who can sustain her.

"You know, even though I've been all over the country, I have rarely met others like us—not enough to know them when I see them, anyway. But you…" I marvel, but then it's too much and I have to look down at my hand and the yellow-ringed shadow it casts on the white sheets. "It's like you've always known, like someone taught you from birth. Who raised you?" I ask. A nervous laugh slips out. "My mother was ashamed of me, ashamed of what we are. She made me feed on animals. All I could take at first was their fucking fear, you know? Like, there was this rabbit that she made me feed on in front of her, and it was so scared and… I didn't know what we could do, what people like us are supposed to do. I mean, how the fuck did I figure it out, right? I didn't know you could feed on people and it wouldn't kill them like it does with animals. I fucking cried the first time."

"Then she gave you nothing," Helene says, and I know what she is picturing: the frail, paranoid person who raised me, fueled entirely by animal fear and instinct. She wouldn't be wrong. "How can she live like that?"

I want to tell her I turned all that shame into rage and killed my mother, sucked all that bitterness and regret out of her body and spit it out as black bile while she withered to leather and bone at my feet, but all I have is the sad truth. "She's dead. Once she decided I was raised, she walked into traffic."

Helene's face tightens, and she appears to take a moment to arrange words that shouldn't be so difficult. "I'm sorry she did that to you," she says, her gaze flicking to my hand on the sheets. "She didn't listen to her instincts, and you paid for that. We're rare, but what we have—that instinct keeps us alive, keeps us strong. It's all we have. And it's never been wrong, has it? It tells us who to take, what to take."

Is this the real reason why I've stayed with the band? Necessity has played a part in selecting every person I've ever fed on, but random desire always led me when I had choices. Isn't that instinct?

I grin. "My instincts led me to you."

She grins too, moves back to the bed. "When you saw me…what were you going to take from me?" she asks.

I think of the first memory I pulled from her, that flash of me dancing in front of the merch table. I'm glad I didn't get a chance to take it; I want her to keep it.

"Your strength," I answer. "Whatever I could take off the top to get me through to the next night."

"Just enough energy so you could fuck me?"

I stretch across the bed and grab both of her hands, pulling her down onto the mattress with me. "More," I say, before my lips find hers.

It's back immediately, the oil and tang of skin filling my mouth, as rich and round as the butter that comes next, the steam, the safety of being wrapped in clean sheets—all the things I tasted when we first kissed. These intrinsic comforts jump to the forefront, something she can afford to share because they've burrowed their way into her DNA; she doesn't have to keep it close to keep it safe. That's what I would take. More than a memory.

So, I ask her.

She tells me about the person who waits for her at home, how she loves Helene in a way Helene doesn't love her. Helene is restless, and she can't control the hunger anymore. That's why she goes to these shows—to feel what I once did—though it's not entirely why she's followed me halfway across the state. She wants to know more about my life on the road, and I want to know more about her woman. How can she be so happy to give Helene all these pieces of herself when Helene's not even dangling the promise of power over her head? Are there people who admire succubi like us? I want to know who raised Helene, or if she's always been this assured. She has an anchor that I cannot consider a heavy weight no matter what she says, and her person is content. It's never occurred to me that I could have that, someone as static and loyal as a place, a home.

"So you've never made anyone before?" I say.

Helene's eyes shift to the door, then back to me. She knows I'm stalling the inevitable. She could tell me everything then slip away at the next rest stop or after I fall asleep, and her secrets would be meaningless because I would never find her again. I didn't even know what she was until it was too late.

After a long moment, she says, "It sounds good, having someone who's always there to give you whatever you need, but it's not good for us, you know? You're the one who got it right, Ronnie. We have to keep moving. Have you ever seen one of us waste away?"

The boys would not waste away without me, but I've always believed we have to keep moving because of them. As I watch Helene walk into the bathroom, I think about what she might take from me tonight, and how I will let her.

5.

I've gone longer without eating, back before I met the band and didn't move around as much, but I've never tested how long I can go without. What shape will I be in when we make it to the next town, the next safe place where the band can play a show and I can lure a drunk fan out behind the club? I'm willing to push it, but I can't hide the hunger, the raw need that loosens the skin from my bones and makes the lines of my body waver and buzz beneath my clothes in a way that I can't dismiss as excitement or nerves. By tomorrow night the boys will know that feeding isn't the reason I brought Helene with us. That's the thing about sharing an 18x6 foot space with four other people day in and day out: they all know what you are trying to hide, and it's just a matter of whether they acknowledge it or not.

While Helene showers, I head out to the vending machines for another kind of sustenance. Sugar and salt are the best I'll get in the middle of night and I'm grateful for it. There's a comfort in having a need that can be fulfilled without attention, without making anyone suffer.

I'm coming back from the lobby with pretzels and a Coke when I see Jack leaned up against the side of the van, smoking a joint.

"Don't ask me what I think of this place," I say, cutting him off as he's opening his mouth.

He laughs and looks down at his feet. The sound is a relief, a lilt of the forgiveness I need. "Guess we can't put roots down now, huh?"

"Fucking Cillian." I sigh.

"He's snoring again," Jack says, flicking the ash from the joint before passing it to me. "He sounds like a fucking plane taking off. I don't know how Sylvy's sleeping through it. Drew's in the tub with a pillow over his face."

"A full meal will do that to you."

"If we had the money we made from merch tonight, we'd be able to get another room."

So he's still mad.

We pass the pretzels and the joint between us. It feels good, that measured inhale then even slower exhale that releases the last of the knots my body's been clenching since Helene and I found the birthday guy dead in the alley. My back slumps against the cold metal of the van and I feel it rock a little away from me. Jack's fingers brush mine every time we pass the joint, him always grabbing close to the cherry so I don't have to risk getting burned. I've told him he doesn't need to do that, but he always smiles and mumbles something about callouses.

I glance at the band's room just a few yards to the left, so quiet and dark, not even a thin line of yellow light outlining the closed curtains. There's a comfort in picturing them in there, safe and contained and four hours away from whoever might have found the dead guy by now. How does Cillian sleep so well? I've been fighting that pang of guilt all night, still regretting that I didn't at least wish the dead guy a happy birthday. *Happy Fucking Birthday, watch out for the guy full of piss and swagger who's been watching you all night.* Perhaps making Cillian wasn't a mistake. Perhaps he's better at this than I am.

Next door is mine and Helene's room. I know I should invite Jack to bunk with us—I want to as much as he wants me to—but I'm not ready for him to know that she's more than a snack, that she's one of us. It's been a long time since there was a wall between the boys and me, but this time it causes me a different kind of worry. Even though I didn't hear Cillian's snoring or even the murmur of their voices through that wall, I worry about what they might have heard when I was with Helene. Telling her about them made me feel vulnerable enough, even without her judgement. Does it matter what they think of her? Under my jacket and my shirt and my jeans I can feel her on my skin like sweat beading in every crease, heat that lingers despite the cold as if she's burned her fingerprints all over my body. Marked me. Can Jack smell her like I can? When he nudges my arm with his, does he feel the buzzing, the hunger? He holds the roach to my mouth for one last puff, and as my lips brush his fingers I wonder if he can feel what I did when I was with Helene, if he will taste the butter, the steam, the long lazy mornings when he brings his fingers to his own lips.

"You're starving," Jack says.

My muscles knot again, and my legs lock under me. I've never been able to hide my hunger from him, just as he has never been able to hide his feelings from me.

"Huh?" I murmur.

I look down at the empty pretzel packet in my hand. My tongue pushes against the build-up of flour and sugar in the crevices of my molars, finds the crystals of salt still nestled against my gums.

"We didn't get our usual pre-show pizza," I say.

Why can't I tell him about Helene? I trust him as much as I've ever trusted anyone. I guess I want her to be mine, just like the band is mine, and the two shouldn't be overlapping.

But they are, in this town nestled in the mountains. We're all tangled up with each other now, perhaps already were the moment the van pulled up to that club somewhere north of Seattle and south of Bellingham.

"You know, you can take what you need from me. I trust you," Jack says, his eyes on his feet again when I turn to look at him. "I mean, if you want some memories, I wouldn't mind you taking this night," he adds with a nervous laugh.

His memories of this night—the adrenaline of loading out faster than we ever have before—would be enough to sustain me until we can safely feed again. I won't lie—I'm tempted. I remember what it was like to be alone in a motel bathroom with him, face pressed into the cold cracked tile, knees aching against the hard bottom of the tub, just drunk enough to lose control of the tunnel that roared open inside me. I took it all: that diminished arpeggio he'd just figured out how to use, his mother teaching him piano chords when he was five, the taste of orange soda and acrid loneliness on the woman he'd had behind the club earlier that night. All of it as thick and toothsome as caramel, filling up my core, but none of it was lasting, every skill and memory fading within days instead of imprinting in my DNA. I was too greedy. Afterward, he was so dazed I had to give him back some of his energy just so he could get out of the tub.

I could do that again. Tonight, I'm not too drunk to control myself. I could take the last four hours of his memories and give him in return the dangerous infatuation that's been swelling in my chest since the night I first saw Helene.

But I don't say anything. Instead, I turn away from Jack and towards my room. There's movement behind the closed curtains, a light turning off then another going on. I picture Helene in a towel, bangs like shards of obsidian plastered to her forehead, as she digs through the bag she had ready in the trunk of her car. Does the woman waiting for her at home know where she is? Does she know if Helene's coming back?

"How long is she staying with us?" Jack asks.

"I don't know," I say.

6.

By the next morning Cillian is bouncing off the walls, fully charged by the energy he drained from the birthday guy. While the rest of us can barely keep our heads off the table, he drinks cup after cup of coffee in the diner down the road from the motel, gesticulating wildly as he talks about how great last night was, how he sang the best he ever has, how the band is a "fucking *machine*." He adds a "you too, Ronnie, we couldn't do it without you" when I sigh audibly. He even lies and tells the waitress that it's his birthday, but her lukewarm "happy birthday" is not the acknowledgement he was hoping for.

We all agree he can't eat again until the next gig.

"When's that gonna be?" he asks. "What about going to a bar tonight? We can do it and get out—no one will notice us." He glances at Helene, who's picking at a stack of pancakes. "Pretty stupid that we do it at the shows we're playing."

"Well, we could do it anywhere if we were more careful," Jack says pointedly. "But by the time people start dropping, we're on stage or back in the van. No one ever suspects the band."

Drew reaches across the table but doesn't quite connect with the carafe of maple syrup. "Can someone pass the syrup?"

"It's get in and get out. You know that," Sylvy says.

"Jack, can you…?" Drew tries again.

Jack pushes a corner of toast around his plate. "We're all hungry, man, okay? Not everyone got as much as you did last night."

32

"What about her?" Cillian says, tipping his head towards Helene and me across the booth.

Jack locks eyes with me in a brief moment no one else seems to notice. Except Helene. While the other guys continue eating, she straightens next to me, making herself bigger, taking up more space as if she's accepting Cillian's challenge. She meets his stare, and I think she might growl, though it would be a waste of energy. With the dark bags under my eyes and the skin loosening around my jaw, I thought it was obvious that I haven't eaten in a couple of days, but it seems Jack's the only one who notices.

"Oh, for fuck sake," Drew mutters, rising so he can make the big reach to the opposite corner of the table. He hovers over my coffee cup, t-shirt clinging to his stomach, and that's when I see the stain, a mottle of dark red, purple, yellowish-green and black—the colors of a bruise in every stage—running from his navel to a pool soaking the hem of his white shirt. A stale, sour odor, like that of the bleached and wizened skin under a bandaid, overtakes the table full of coffees and bacon and breakfast sweets.

"Drew," I say as he's sliding back down in the booth, syrup carafe in hand. "What is that?"

"What?"

"On your shirt. That stain."

Everyone's attention swings to Drew as he looks down at himself. Next to him, Cillian's eyes widen and he drops a forkful of eggs back onto his plate.

"Dude, what is that?"

Drew focuses on pouring syrup over his pancakes, his other arm folded over his stomach. "What? Nothing."

"That is *not* nothing," Cillian says, his hand creeping towards Drew.

Drew puts the carafe down and uses it to nudge Cillian's hand until he retreats.

"Fuck, did that just happen, like while we've been sitting here?" Sylvy asks, reaching across Cillain. Drew swats his hand away too. "'Cuz we would've noticed that." He looks at me. "You would've noticed that, right?"

"It's kinda hard not to," I agree.

Drew folds his other arm in front of himself, then winces and readjusts so that both arms are encircling his middle without actually touching it. "I must've spilled something."

We all glance around the table. "It looks like your bellybutton puked," Cillian says.

Helene looks at me. Her jaw is suddenly soft, her bottom lip dropped in a held-breath. She looks like she might be sick.

"I'm gonna go back to the room and change my shirt," Drew announces. He starts to stand, but Cillian snags him by the shirt hem. The fabric pulls away from Drew's stomach, making a whispered tearing sound, a crackle like breaking the seal of dried blood against skin. Drew winces. Underneath, his stomach is stained the same as his shirt, his navel strangely elongated—gaping—and filled with a dark, murky liquid that has congealed there.

"Fuckin' get your hand off me," Drew snaps, slumping back into his seat.

Jack's eyes widen with a concern that outweighs any previous friction. "What happened to you? You look like you've been stabbed."

"That looks like an infected bellybutton piercing," Cillian adds.

My gut clenches around the knot forming there, that dropped-bottom seed of instinct that something is not right.

Despite what must be some terrible pain, Drew doesn't look feverish or wan; I never would have suspected something was wrong with him if I hadn't seen that stain. How could I have missed this? I made these guys, but the cord was cut as soon as our bodies parted. I'm no more their mother than the van or the road or every promoter who's thrown a six pack our way.

Helene's words drift though my head: *You made them, but they don t belong to you, and you don t belong to them. They re not your purpose, Ronnie.*

"I'm fine, okay?" Drew says. "I just need to change my shirt."

Helene swallows, a sound both dry and sticky, and she draws her features back into set, composed lines. "How long has your stomach been like that?"

"I said it's fine. I just cut myself."

"How the fuck do you cut your bellybutton?" Cillian marvels. *Bellybutton.* This time when Cillian says it, the word is more grave than ridiculous.

Drew shoves a forkful of pancakes into his mouth and stands, syrup oozing from the corner of his mouth as he chews. "We gotta get going. We have calls to make."

"That looks infected," Jack says. "We should stop at an urgent care."

"Seriously, you need to have that looked at," I agree.

"I said I'm *fine.*"

Helene stands too. "He's right. It's almost checkout time. We should get out of here."

Everyone rushes to get what's left on their plates into their mouths, though they all look a little nauseous as if they now smell Drew's wound too. Drew keeps an arm over his middle, then both arms when the waitress brings the check. All I can do is say his name, but it comes out as a hoarse warble.

"There's an old first aid kit in the van," Jack says, and that is enough for everyone.

Helene pays the check. I know I should, but I don't say anything, and neither do the other guys.

Back in the motel's parking lot, after we've loaded up the van and checked out, the boys make their calls and texts while Helene and I wait in her car. Drew, in a clean shirt, calls the promoter in Vancouver, but I can tell it doesn't go well by how he hurls his phone into the van. Jack and Sylvy look as disappointed as I am that we won't be going back to British Columbia any time soon, though it would be stupid to anyway, with the dead body we left behind so close to the border. The boys pace and argue, fingers flying over their phones as they make promises and try to cash in favors that will land us somewhere east of Washington tonight if we're lucky. I'm so fucking hungry. I could pull Jack, Sylvy, Drew and Cillian into the back of the van now, take their memories of last night and this miserable morning from them, and we would all be okay, we would all get what we need.

"You've never seen that before?" Helene asks as she's scrolling through her phone. She's scanning news sites, every regional paper from west to east.

"Drew's stomach? No, but I don't believe he cut himself either. He probably got bit by whomever he last fed on and he's too embarrassed to admit it," I say.

"He's sick."

I turn on the radio and scan the AM stations, pausing at anything that sounds like local news. Traveling with the band these last six years, I've seen plenty of gross stuff, and whatever is going on with Drew's navel falls squarely in the middle between witnessing Sylvy piss in a soda cup in the back of the van and helping Cillian clean the blood and vomit out of his hair after a feeding gone wrong. There's been worse, there will be worse. Despite that ominous feeling in my gut back at the diner, right now I have to be more concerned about the dead birthday guy.

"The guys got him bandaged up. We'll get him to an urgent care," I tell Helene, straining to hear a voice in the radio static.

"No, you can't. He's—"

"Wait. Here's something."

We both stare at the radio. A man found dead in his car in south Seattle, nowhere near where we played last night. I keep scanning. We're silent through every snippet of town meetings and high school football games, but we don't hear anything about any other bodies found last night.

"You ever think about the people we feed on, how they are afterwards?" I ask Helene.

"Sure." She flicks off the radio and turns back to her phone. "I don't worry about it, if that's what you mean. I know how to control myself."

"Sometimes I think we're doing them a favor, or we *should* be doing them a favor, taking the bad stuff, their memories of the worst parts of their night."

She's scrolling through her phone again, face pinched as she flips between news sites. I recognize the same photos, the same headlines, articles she's already looked at. "You can't do that," she says. "If you only take the bad shit, it's like eating poison."

So what does she take from her person at home? Why would she give herself to Helene if all she leaves her with are memory gaps and weakness?

"What were you saying about—" I start to ask, but I'm interrupted by my phone's chime. It's a text from Jack: *Spokane tomorrow night. $700 guarantee.*

I tell Helene. She returns her phone to her pocket and starts the car.

7.

We have more than twenty-four hours to kill before the show in Spokane. Drew, much more buoyant than he was this morning, floats the idea of playing an impromptu set at whatever dive will have us tonight—"hell, we can do it for free drinks, make a little money off some merch"— but whatever little money we make will barely be enough for gas to the next place. It's not worth the risk. We have to lay low, even if that means sleeping in the van in a Wal-Mart parking lot for the night.

The band has gone on hiatus before, after someone ends up dead. I'm always waiting for someone to put it together, some detective or grieving family member to match our tour schedule to where the bodies turn up and notice that the next show or two gets cancelled before we're playing again two states away. The last time someone died—it was Sylvy that time; the guy he fed off had a seizure right there in the pit during the encore—I got them to play the next show as scheduled just thirty miles away, acting like nothing happened because we had to believe we were innocent; it's not our fault if someone with a medical condition collapses at a show. And that's the thing, why the boys don't worry as much as I do: every dead person we've left in our wake has died without a mark on them, just a stopped heart and empty eyes, and a body so worn a time of death can't be pinpointed. I should trust as Cillian does that the birthday guy's death will be blamed on drugs or alcohol or an undiagnosed heart condition. Despite the fact that the guy was found wedged behind a dumpster, there likely won't be enough questions to warrant further investigation.

Still, no one eats until after the show tomorrow night. I make that clear, and despite the skin I see loosening around Jack's eyes, he backs me up. Drew and Sylvy agree that they can bear a day without feeding, probably because my hunger is visible to them now and they know I've gone much longer. They all eye Helene, though, and I'm scared that they're wondering why I'm abstaining when I have her.

Or are they wondering why I don't share her?

Still, no one argues. Even Cillian doesn't utter more than a low grumble. I want it to be because of guilt, but it's probably because he's still full from the birthday guy.

I'm so fucking hungry I can't think straight. Then Helene reminds me that it doesn't have to be this way.

To assuage my guilt, Helene pays for two motel rooms off US 2 just outside of Spokane. It's decent—we've certainly stayed in worse places over the years—with HBO and three treadmills crammed in a closet they call the fitness center, more than we usually have to occupy ourselves on a night in. There's even a coin laundry, and I'm nearly giddy that for the first time in weeks I won't have to wash my underwear in the bathroom sink. The boys are suspicious, but they don't argue, not after Helene offers a little ketamine too. I don't know where her money comes from, and I don't ask. Once the boys are settled in, whisky-pliant and talking about writing some new music as the night slips down around us, Helene and I head out into town.

We drive up and down a broad network of city blocks, following the loose clots of people flocking to the warmth glowing behind glass storefronts set in red brick. I point to a place lit only by votives, the orange faces inside throbbing in and out of view, but Helene doesn't want to hunt in the dark. We look too good, she says, and she's right. It felt good to put on something sexy, to take our time getting ready as we bumped shoulders in the motel bathroom's mirror. It was a thrill to slip out to Helene's unassuming black sedan, eyes darting to the open window of the room next door where Cillian, Jack, Drew and Sylvy were already enveloped in each other, guitars and bass passing between them as the ketamine took hold. Without the boys, I can take all night to hunt instead of grabbing whomever I can seduce the fastest. Tonight will be a sumptuous feast, discerning and languorous, a rare treat that won't be marred by the indignity of scarfing down whatever's left in an alley or a filthy bathroom while the boys are loading out.

Under the unforgiving fluorescents of a sports bar, Helene and I are invisible to the men gathered inside, erased by the younger women playing pool and looking for the same thing those men are. I'm all too aware of the eyeliner settling into the creases around my eyes, the way the hunger slackens the line of my jaw and betrays my age. Helene doesn't seem to mind, though, her gaze as undaunted as her fingers sliding up and down my thigh under the table. After a round of beers we move on to a candlelit den where we spend an hour sipping bourbon neat and laughing quietly, and she turns my hand over in hers as if we are on a romantic date like the other couples huddled together around us. For a short time it's enough to push the hunger back, and I'm sure there is a poet out there that could tell you all about how love is food is air.

Love. Fuck. All this drinking on an empty stomach has gone to my head.

The hunger roars back when we're out on the sidewalk again. I think about Drew, that foul substance leaking out of his gaping navel, and I fear the cramp that seizes my own stomach, though I know it's nothing more than the ache of my angry, hungry core. Helene holds me close as if she's trying to absorb all of my wavering lines, somehow squeeze them out of my thin skin and divide the ache between the two of us. When she presses her mouth to mine I feel that tunnel in me stretch wide open and I'm afraid I can't control myself, but she doesn't let go of me. She opens up too, but, unlike the night we met, she is pushing into me, encouraging that pull, that *up up up* I've already given in to, offering me a memory of slender fingers—a woman's hand; her woman's fingers?—digging into her forearm. A rush of adrenaline floods my limbs and seizes the back of my neck.

I turn my head just in time to spew a string of gasping coughs into her neck. Everything's sun-bleached and sparking behind my squeezed-shut eyes, my stomach violently retching as if trying to expel the bitter heat I just tasted. I push Helene back harder than I mean to, but she doesn't look angry or surprised.

"You need this," she says, wiping my saliva from her neck. "Don't be a martyr."

My nose is running and I'm shaking again, so we walk a couple of blocks in the crisp night air, watching small clumps of people dwindle down to singles, then no one at all. Whatever Helene gave me did the trick, though, and I can feel my skin plumping and my lines smoothing out as we approach another bar. It's in this third bar, under exposed ductwork and the sweat of blue lights that remind me of the venues I know so well, that our luck begins.

We snag the last seats in the place, in a cozy corner booth that Helene claims in a blur of black on black and a "fuck you" aura that keeps the other hovering people at bay. There's a good mix here tonight, a nice balanced representation of people in their twenties through forties who look just the right amount of willing. I see strong bodies, full bellies, pleasant memories being made tonight. And they're all just tipsy enough to be friendly, but not so drunk they'll make a scene when Helene and I lead them through the crowd and out into the cold, empty night.

While I'm at the bar waiting for our drinks, I watch a couple of middle-aged men approach Helene, then quickly leave with their mouths shaped into the word "bitch". This happens with another pair of men, then a single guy. Her allure, her beauty, allow her to be choosy, but this bar is not dark enough to hide the deep lines hunger has carved on my face. I need her to hook someone first, to pull them in enough that they won't pull back when I join her. Without the proximity of the band, will anyone want me when there are other choices and the night is far from ending?

I've got our drinks in hand when a new pair approaches Helene, a couple of women who look like they haven't seen a night out in a long time. She rebuffs them just as quickly, and I watch the women pick their way to another table, nothing but the softest arcs as they lean and whisper and clutch each other awkwardly. I imagine husbands at home waiting up for these women, men content to tend fat babies and make turkey sandwiches pinned with love notes and the hope that momma had fun. These women are the warm sheets, the honey and butter, the safety of walking through the same door every night. It takes everything I have to keep myself from sweeping these women into the alley and devouring them whole.

"What the fuck?" I say to Helene, plopping two gin and tonics on our table. "What was wrong with those women?"

"You need more. You need better," Helene says, tipping her head towards the entrance.

A man and a woman, so young they make my teeth itch, are hovering near the exit, clutching beers, necks arching and heads swiveling as they search for somewhere to settle. They look in opposite directions, then their gazes come together and zero in on Helene and me and all the extra space in our booth. I turn to Helene. She is staring at them—open, bold, inviting—and then she smiles just as she did the first time I saw her.

They are Rachel and Caleb, best friends from high school. Rachel is home for her grandmother's funeral, then it's back to UCLA before the next quarter starts. I'm bored by the introductions, but Helene leans into the awkward pauses and nervous giggles. "What are you studying, Rachel?" she asks, the *E* and *L* unfurling as smooth as caramel. "What do you like to do when you're not working, Caleb?" His name puffs on her lips. "Rachel," Helene says, the subtle roar of the *R* blooming heat from my lower back to my thighs. "Rachel, do you always drink stouts?" "Caleb." She punctures the air with the soft and wet smack of the *B*. "Caleb, what's fun to do around here?"

Rachel and Caleb giggle. They preen. I can feel the tremble of excitement that seeps from their fingertips onto the table top, just enough to disrupt the surface of my drink. Helene's fingers flutter over her own empty glass and Caleb is up immediately with the promise of another round.

What do they think they will get from us? Certainly not free drinks. Maybe it's a cool-aunt kind of attraction. Caleb wants to fuck Helene, but Rachel is a little more

44

reserved, reflecting my own reservations. I just hope they don't see us as a novelty, a story of the night they spent with a couple of horny rock and roll hags. I won't be the go-to punchline at house parties and high school reunions.

"Ronnie here is in a band," Helene says when Caleb returns with tequila shots.

"Oh, yeah? Anyone I know?"

"She's in the—" Helene's expression hops when I kick her under the table, and she covers with an easy laugh. "She sings," she tell them.

"That's cool," Rachel says. "What kind of music?"

I give Helene a look, but she's turned that soft, open gaze to me now, a game that could be as gentle or harsh as I want. "Mostly rock. Some hard stuff. Sometimes psychobilly," I answer.

"Cool," Caleb says, dropping his Os and rolling them out. He either doesn't care or has no fucking idea what I just said.

"Her band's playing a show here tomorrow night." Helene turns to me. "It's at the Rundown, right? You guys should come. We'll put you on the list."

I dig my fingers into her thigh under the table, but she doesn't flinch. She's pushing me, sealing this deal. There will be no going back tonight.

I'm afraid we're losing Rachel and Caleb, but it's easy for Helene to keep them hooked and sinking under her gaze. Every time she says their names I remember how it felt when all those suede-plush Os and Ns of my own name melted off her tongue and into my ears. How she didn't have to ask my name again, as if she liked the way it felt in her mouth. How she made me feel like I was the only person in the room. Her focus, like fingers burrowing deep into me and unlatching a door I'd spent years barricading.

And it looks just the same, what she's giving these kids. Is this how she always operates? Was I just prey? But she stayed. She followed me across the state. Unlike with these kids, she hasn't taken a damn thing from me.

Helene asks the kids more questions about themselves and they run wild with the opportunity as if no one has ever listened before. But Helene is not listening, and neither am I. I'm watching their lips as they speak, their fingers flexing and drawing lines in the air as their excitement grows. I'm imagining what they taste like. Rachel, the college junior, bursting with the memories of so many firsts and the wonder of fresh knowledge. Caleb, with his dream to build a cabin in the wilds of West Virginia, or is it Wyoming? I could use a dose of that hope and ambition to sweeten more than my tongue.

Soon we're outside, all four of us a little drunk and the two kids looser than they should be. Caleb knows another place, somewhere dark and quiet, so we pile into his SUV, Helene and him in the front and Rachel and me in the back. Rachel squeezes my hand. Caleb's checking his phone, and I'm still wondering what these kids want from us. Do they think they're in control? Do they think that Helene and I aren't dangerous because we're women?

Helene turns around in the front seat and grins at me. When I lean forward, she grabs my face with both hands and kisses me. Then she turns to Caleb and starts kissing him.

Rachel's eyes and mouth widen into fat, glossy rings and she looks at me as if to verify what she is seeing. She starts to giggle. I slide my hand around the back of her neck and close my mouth over hers.

So many firsts tonight. Too bad they won't remember any of this.

Rachel is as sweet as I expected, and from the noises Helene is making in the front seat, it sounds like Caleb is too. As the tunnel roars open—I can't help it; I want to take my time and enjoy this, but I'm so fucking hungry—Rachel leans into me as if she can't help herself either. She is so young, and I could so easily take her past and all the years she has left. I try to be selective, though, and control myself and what I take: a few months she'll barely miss, but enough to plump my skin and undo so many nights of too much gin and vomiting in the van; a memory of a fight with her roommate, so sharp and exhilarating when she realized how easy it would be to hit someone; the taste of melted chocolate imprinted on her tongue. I pull it all up out of her and into myself. I take my time until I feel my body strengthen and the prickly spike of hunger wear down to nothing. As Rachel goes limp in my arms, I finish by taking every memory she's made of Helene and me, carefully sipping from her mind until all she has left is Caleb and a lovely evening in a big booth they had all to themselves.

Helene, already finished with Caleb, is watching me. Her smile is all mine again. We leave the kids in their SUV parked on an empty side street, slumped like a couple of over-served lightweights sleeping off a buzz.

In her car, she gives me a little bit of Caleb and I give her a little bit of Rachel. So much trust and confidence and optimism, all as smooth as bourbon and as verdant as gin. It braids together everything in me that's been frayed from the past few days; I feel like I've been dipped in wax, a coating that will be just as satisfying to crack whenever this ecstasy wears off. I see the night from Caleb's and Rachel's point of view, and I think of the song the boys wrote for me, the one they play at every show. Helene and I are fascinating. We are beautiful.

And I am full. So deliciously, luxuriously full.

When we get back to the motel, Jack is smoking under the dingy yellow funnel of light illuminating the ice machine. He watches Helene and me pour out of her car, hands fumbling to find each other when we meet again on the walkway to our room. I can't stop smiling. I can't stop laughing. My skin is smooth and plump, my movements are wide and confident. Satisfied. It feels good to be seen, and I don't care that Jack sees me like this. Sees us. I blow him a kiss as Helene sweeps me inside our room.

Being full like this—so utterly satisfied—for the first time in months is intoxicating, better than the far away float of a K-hole or the warm sinking of alcohol. The thing is, I'm not numb; in fact, I feel everything as if for the first time, as if my skin is stretched so that the secret parts of me are exposed and proud and greedily drinking in Helene's every touch. My bones vibrate as she pulls off my clothes. My fingertips hum and spark along all her smooth lines. We're fat with youth and optimism and boundless possibility. I've never been so confident, so content, while standing naked in front of another person in my life.

It's not until I'm drifting off to sleep next to Helene that Rachel and Caleb creep into my thoughts. I keep wondering what they will think when they wake up in his car as the sun comes up. I wonder if their confusion will be pricked by a moment of fear—same as the pinch of guilt that now nips at the back of my head—as they realize something is different.

8.

"So, how was your night?" Jack asks, passing me the joint. He thinks I need a hangover balm. He's not wrong.

"You know." I take a hit and pass it back to him. I roll the van's window halfway down so we're not the idiots hotboxing in the motel parking lot. "I went without eating a lot longer than you guys. We were careful. You know I'm careful."

He blows a plume of smoke into the windshield and the inside of the van goes as white as the rainy sky outside. "I know."

"How's Drew?"

Jack shrugs. "Okay, I guess. He says it's not infected."

"How would he know? He's not a doctor. I thought we were taking him to urgent care."

"He doesn't want to go. Not like we can afford it anyway."

That would have been true in any situation, but today it feels like a little dig, a reminder that I lost our earnings from the last show. "Someone bit him, and he doesn't want to have to explain that to a doctor," I say. "Remember that time that guy puked all over Cillian's head while he was blowing him?"

"What was it? Like vodka and grape cough syrup? And he kept going until the guy started puking up blood."

"He was more pissed that the guy ruined his perfect hair day."

We share a laugh. Soon the joint's done, Jack giving me two hits in a row then taking the last one as the cherry nips his fingers. We're parked facing our rooms. Both windows are still dark, the curtains drawn. I left Helene asleep in bed when Jack tapped on my window, coffee in hand, just after ten a.m.

"You seem happy," he says, staring straight ahead.

I try to resist, but a little smile twitches my lips.

"So, what do you think of—"

"Don't even," I cut him off. He smiles.

Even the smallest movements make the coffee slosh in my stomach, and I can't imagine stuffing some pancakes in there even if it would settle things. Last night—that slow, sumptuous feast with Helene—really was enough. I feel swollen all over, but in a good way. It's warm and soft. I could settle here, but not in the way Jack wants.

"We can't do this forever, Ronnie," Jack says, but the *O* and *N*s aren't cream and caramel on his tongue. He gives a rueful little laugh. "We're getting old."

"Rock and roll never gets old."

"You know what I mean. I can't see myself standing on a stage in some shithole when I'm sixty-five. Can you?" He turns in the driver's seat so that he's facing me and he looks warm and soft too, but not in a good way; the ketamine comedown weighs heavy in his jaw and limbs. "I can't imagine myself still picking off drunks who wandered away from their friends and scarfing them down in bathrooms and alleys like we're a bunch of fucking stray cats," he says, curling both arms over his stomach. "I'm tired, Ronnie, and I know you're tired too."

"We stay and we get caught. We have to keep moving. There's no choice," I remind him, words I've said so many times that they sound hollow.

Jack turns his gaze back out the windshield. No one noticed my absence and Jack's absence, I'm certain of it. Not beyond Drew or Helene stretching out in bed and finding more warm space to claim as their own.

"You could settle down with her," Jack says as if my last words are meaningless to him. "She knows what you are and she's still here. We've been all over this country ten times over. Remember that little mountain town outside of Denver? You loved it there." When I don't say anything, he shakes his head and his mouth pulls tight. "You think about the people we feed on, don't you? I didn't at first, but now I do all the time. It feels so fucking good, then it feels like shit right after."

"Where is this coming from? I didn't see you having a moral crisis when—" I stop myself. I don't know why. "We're doing what we're supposed to do, what we have to do," I say.

Face set hard, he turns back to me and for a moment I'm a monster on the playground again, getting too close, moving too fast, dodging rocks and names from the kids who knew what I was before I did.

He shifts in his seat, and I'm a little girl under my mother's glare again, crying over the rabbit I drained dead while she told me to suck it up.

Jack's eyes were the same as that rabbit's the night he and I met, hard and black with fear. It was so beautiful staring into his eyes, the way his pupils bloomed into endless velvet as I made him.

"These people, we never ask them," he says. "They have no idea what we're going to do to them. We take things from them we have no right to take." I start to open my mouth, but he continues. "You can tell yourself all you want that we're taking the bad stuff, all the bad memories they have of that night, but we don't have any fucking right to do that either. Never mind taking their strength, or their talent, or their youth. It's never *just* a taste."

I throw my hands up. "Then what the fuck are we supposed to do, Jack? Starve? We can't fucking help who we are."

Well, I could have. I could've helped who he—they—became.

"How many of us are there, people like us? You know there's got to be people who are into it, who would consent," he says. "Everybody gets what they want. We could settle down with someone like that. We could live the rest of our lives that way."

Has he been talking to Helene? Is that what he thinks she is?

"Then that's it, that's how we live? I don't want to be some dirty secret," I say.

"We already are."

Jack's still irritated when I leave him in the van and go back to my room. Helene is exactly as I left her, curled with her back to me, comforter kicked off and sheets pulled up to her chin. I ease my way back into bed so as not to disturb her, but she rolls over before I can get all the way under the sheets. She doesn't open her eyes. Her smell is thick in the air, juniper and peppercorns, woodsmoke in her hair, and the musk of drawn limbs heavy with sleep. As I turn away from her, I feel her arm slide over my side until her hand finds its way under my t-shirt. She pulls me close and holds me there, one hand on my stomach and the other folded in the small of my back. Her nose burrows into the nape of my neck. I smell like cheap weed and booze sweat, but she doesn't seem to care. She sighs.

It's been a long time since I've slept with someone like this. Sleeping alone has been my sole contribution to the tour rider, a line the boys don't cross, a badge of honor some days, and a guilty burden on others. When you spend half your life in an 18x6 van, you have to carve out whatever space of your own you can. But here I am. This is my time, there is plenty of space in this bed, but I don't want any of it. All I want is for Helene to keep holding me.

9.

Even the soundcheck is shitty.

The promoter has us come an hour before the doors open. We load in, Helene and I with the merch and the boys with their gear. Everyone's got just enough in them for a few pleasantries with the opening band, who are already drinking at the bar. Not even a beer in him and Cillian looks like he's ready to beat his feedback-ridden mic into Jack's amp if only he had the strength. The sound guy can't figure out the extra pickup for Drew's standup bass. He gives a pointed sigh as he waits for Sylvy to set up his pedal, snare and cymbals. By the time all the mics and monitors have been tested and they get to playing an actual song, the sound guy looks ready to quit and the promoter looks like he already regrets booking the band.

Drew reminds everyone that the promoter is doing us a favor, so they can't play like shit tonight. Doesn't matter that no one here cares for the headlining band. Doesn't matter that we already got our guarantee. We have to sell albums and shirts. They have to play like they fucking own this stage, this town. *No matter what.*

It's clearest on Cillian's face: *No matter that we haven't eaten. No matter that we're starving.*

The green room's being occupied by the headlining band and no one's got it in them to fight, so the boys mill around the empty bar as people start trickling in for the pre-show happy hour. Free well drinks and rider-fulfilling pizza don't make anyone less crabby, but at least there's an edge to the moodiness, a sign of life. Cillian tries to nap in a booth, one eye popping open every time someone ventures nearby as if he's in a constant state of meal planning. Jack sits across from him, but he won't be able to stop Cillian with the way he's nodding off. When the promoter gives me shit about sitting behind the merch table—"This area's for the band; you can't be here, ma'am"—Drew and Sylvy step in before I can tell the guy to go fuck himself. We all could afford a little fight, just not with each other.

Still, whenever I'm in earshot, everyone has a barbed little comment about how *tired* they are, how they hope they don't fuck up tonight.

I'm pretty sure it's more the ketamine comedown than hunger, but there's no point in telling them that. Still, it doesn't sting any less. I fluctuate between dismissing my boys as spoiled, and being pecked by the guilt that comes from not providing for them. If I'm their mother—it doesn't matter if I don't see myself that way; I made them, I worry about them, they come to me for comfort—then I'm in charge and they have to respect that. Why should I feel guilty that, for once, my belly is full? How many nights did I go without eating so that they would have enough? After Cillian willfully drained the birthday guy, it's clear that I've been too slack, too easy on these boys. I've held those hands and they've bitten mine. It's time they learn how to live with real hunger.

At least they're listening to me, despite the resentment that threatens to eclipse the hunger and make our night shitty no matter what I do. They are keeping their promise. I hope Helene is seeing this, even if it is marred.

Sylvy gets weird first. The Cramps' "Queen of Pain" comes on the PA and he comes up behind me while I'm talking to the bartender. He slips his arms around me from behind, spins me to face him, then rolls me out on the end of his arm as Lux Interior draws out "pain". The bartender rolls her eyes. Sylvy's movements chop through the space between us with the churn of the guitars. He snaps me back to him on every one of Lux's hard *T*s. "Very cute," I say, but Sylvy just smiles and gives me another spin. He's done this before—they all have—when I've been angry and he wanted to change that. I know it's not much more than manipulation, but—maybe because I'm still filled with Rachel's optimism—I want it to work. I don't want them to be hungry anymore. I want to be taken back to those exhilarating early days after I first met the band and I saw how this could last forever. Any one of those guys shakes me up, makes me laugh, and I'm there again. I'm reminded of exactly why I made them.

Except it's a little different with Sylvy this time. At Ivy's guitar solo he slides behind me, rubbing up the length of my body from hips to shoulders. He nudges my hair to the side and I feel his nose brush against the back of my neck, then his lips, then his tongue. A dart. A bump. Just a taste. When I turn around he pulls me to him, closing every gap I manage. He is manic and delirious at the same time. His focused, glassy-eyed gaze reminds me of Helene's on the night I first saw her.

I recognize that need. He knows I do. He also knows that the last time I fed him, he vomited everything I gave and was sick for days.

The boys have been getting worse in recent months, seething with uncontrolled hunger after barely a day without eating. I used to think they were spoiled and greedy, but now I'm not so sure.

It's almost enough to break my resolve.

As the Cramps transition to the Gutter Twins, I look around the venue. Cillian is laid out flat in the booth now. Jack is still bent over his phone, back to me. Drew is at the bar chatting up a woman who may be his post-show meal. There are only ten or so other people here, and none of them are looking at Sylvy and me, or they're choosing to ignore the spectacle he's making. I don't see Helene anywhere.

Sylvy's still got me close, one hand on the small of my back and the other clutching my right hand against his chest as if we're forcing a slow dance on the wrong song. I give in and rest my head on his shoulder. The restless lines of his body jump against my cheek. It feels good, and I feel guilty.

They will play like shit tonight. No one will buy merch. The promoter will never work with us again.

Why let all that happen? With what's left of Rachel and Caleb still buzzing in my veins, is it cruel to cling to this bit of control?

A burnt blue shaft of dusk cuts through the center of the bar as the door opens and Helene walks in from outside. She orders a drink, then takes a seat at the merch table. She smiles at me. Cillian sits up. Jack turns to follow his gaze. Drew stops talking to the woman at the bar. Everyone is looking at Helene with that open, rapt desire, but she doesn't seem to care.

Sylvy releases me; he too is helpless to her axis, as weak to the hunger as he is from it.

"Okay," I tell him. "Just a little. Just enough to get through the set."

My acquiescence ignites a flame in Sylvy's eyes. He's on me fast, big hands cupping my face, thumbs pushing up under my jaw so that I'm forced to stand on my tiptoes. His mouth meets mine in a kiss first; even if it's nothing more than propriety, I appreciate the moment to gather what I want to give him.

Once I feel his pull—the tunnel roaring open deep in his core sending waves of suction into my mouth and down my throat—I have only seconds to cement my own control. I open up just enough to allow a bit of Rachel's youthful energy—all I'm willing to give him—to be pulled out of my own core without resistance. I feel that sizzle and spark I have not yet fully absorbed race over my tongue and onto Sylvy's. The music all around us swells, Sylvy's grip on me relaxes, and when I open my eyes I'm able to pull back enough to see his are still closed, his lips vibrating with a growl that matches Mark Lanegan's pouring out of the speakers overhead.

His arms may be sore in the morning, but he'll get through the set. There's even enough for him to share with the other boys if they can get some privacy in the green room.

Except it's not enough.

I can't even take a step back before Sylvy's on me again, hands clutching my upper arms, mouth pressing into my mine, relentlessly bearing down on me even as I bend my head so far back I think my throat's going to split. He's pulling and I'm blown open. *Up up up* goes months of warm milk and storybook tuck-ins, the taste of melted chocolate, watching a campfire on a blanket under the stars—so much of Rachel's youth that I already broke down and processed so it might as well be my own. Sylvy squeezes and there is no room to push or kick. In my mind I'm screaming and flailing, but I know that to everyone else in this bar, we just look like passionate lovers.

Then it's over just as abruptly. Something wrenches Sylvy backwards and I fall out of his grip and double over as I struggle to catch my breath. My lips are numb and my gums itch. Nausea washes down the back of my throat and hollows out my stomach. Hands braced on my thighs, I wait for my vision to focus. How much did he take? Will I be worse off than I was before I ate? A blur of black and white sharpens in front of me. It's Sylvy, flat on his ass on the floor, panting, staring at something behind me as if he can't believe what just happened. I would turn around, except I can't take my eyes off his torso, shirt hiked up, stomach exposed, navel dribbling dark, murky liquid over the top of his jeans.

The sour odor of moist, wizened skin rises up between us. Just like with Drew.

I feel a hand on my back as I straighten. It's Helene. "Let's get some air," she says, but she's not looking at me. She's focused on Sylvy, her eyes narrowed and her features drawn into vicious lines, a warning that everyone in the place can see.

I can tell Sylvy is sorry by the way he keeps looking at me; no matter where we are in the venue, he eyes me not with naked hunger but with a glassy gaze and that held-breath lift in his chest of something we wants—*needs*—to say but can't get out. At times Helene has that same look, but she brushes it off when I ask. If she has something to apologize for, I don't want to know, not right now.

Sylvy buys me drinks, but Helene cuts him off at every approach. We sit behind the merch table and each drink one of his gifted G&Ts, her with her legs crossed and a knowing glare over the rim of her glass. They even have some words right before the opening band goes on. Helene draws a hard line that I've never attempted, that I've never thought I could, as if I owe these guys for changing them into something powerful. Predators. Sylvy stands up to her, but it doesn't last long; he's like a cat, quivering under all that hissing and spitting.

No wonder the band is so spoiled. They don't need to control themselves when they have me.

Sylvy rushes to the bathroom a couple of times, presumably to vomit, hopefully to clean up his stomach. He didn't get bitten by a previous meal too, did he? I wonder if whatever Drew's got—his likely bite wound, his possible infection—is contagious. As the boys drift around the venue, I find myself watching them, anxious every time they stand too close to each other. Helene saw what I saw, but her sympathy is as thin as her tolerance.

In the women's room I pull up my shirt and examine my stomach in the mirror. Sylvy touched me. His body was pressed against mine. He kissed me. And now he's got what Drew's got. In the low light I squint at my reflection. My skin is clean and dry. I press my finger into my navel, but find it sealed as it's always been.

Sylvy is emotionally wounded, but appears physically fine. Both he and Drew joke around with the other guys and shoot their usual hungry looks at the strangers they intend to dine on after the show. I want to tell them I'm okay, that despite what Sylvy took I don't feel sick or weak—just embarrassed, really, that I gave in so easily, that I let him take advantage of me, that Helene had to rescue me and I liked it—but I can't hold a conversation with the images flashing though my mind. Every time Drew's close I smell that stale, sour odor again, and I imagine that split in his navel spreading, an angry, ragged fissure down his pelvis, his liquified guts seeping out as his core, his tunnel—the thing that makes him what he is—rots from the inside out.

10.

People start pouring in at the end of the opening band's set, that "fashionably late" tenet that defines everything from parties to rock shows. They're all so young, these fans or bored kids, as if every family in the tri-city area sent their fifteen to twenty-two-year-olds so mom and dad could have a night in. It's a good thing, though: kids are usually willing to spend money, and they're spending tonight. I sell over $300 worth of t-shirts and albums before the band even goes on stage.

Sylvy must have shared what I gave him because the band does not play like shit. They're actually good, returning the energy of the crowd despite the weariness that drags down their limbs as the night wears on. Cillian is full of piss and banter. Drew spins his stand-up bass like a dance partner. Even Jack and Sylvy look like they're having a good time. People keep pouring in, bodies threading through every space, haloed by a mist of spit as they yell and laugh and sing along. They deliver armloads of longneck beers to the stage, the same as coins in a jukebox. The venue throbs, the walls flexing and bloated with sweat and the collective voices of fans who know every word of every chorus.

Helene and I enjoy ourselves between merch sales. The metronome bass of one of the band's rockabilly numbers guides my hips, swings my body into rhythm with Helene's. During a slower song she holds me close, and though I appreciate this moment to breathe, there's that prick in the back of my neck that reminds me that others are watching us, that people already saw her pull Sylvy off me, that she stands out even when she isn't swaying against me. We can't be sure we're in a safe space; we never know if the men approaching us want to fuck us or punish us for being two women touching each other in this way.

She must feel me stiffen, because she lets her hands slide down my arms and creates space between us. I'm afraid I've hurt her, but she gives me a soft smile and seamlessly moves into dancing on her own. While she's watching the band, I scan the crowd. We are invisible, and if we are not, we will be gone from this place soon enough.

We will eat elsewhere. We will be careful to feed on only the opposite sex as the band and I have done in the towns and liminal spaces that made us unsure.

"Fuck it!" I scream into the vortex of guitar and bass and drums and other voices much louder than my own.

When I slide back into Helene's orbit, she looks pleasantly surprised, but she doesn't miss a beat. She drapes her long arms atop my shoulders and I let my hands find her hips. Cillian's croon burrows into my spine, guiding me closer to Helene. She smells like the air outside, when it's bloated just before the crack of thunder. On my tongue, the hollow of her throat tastes of salt and burnt almonds.

I can see it in the way she watches the band, then in the shy smile she gives me when she catches me watching her. I can feel it in the way her fingers caress the back of my neck, the way her boots tap uncontrollably against the concrete floor: she sees why I did what I did, why I love this band.

We're still pressed together like this when the song ends and Cillian is panting his *thank you*s.

"We've got one more tonight," he announces over the crowd's growing roar. The audience knows what song it is—I know what song it is—before Jack even plays the first bars.

My moment. I want Helene to hear this, to know that this is for me.

Who doesn't get a little wild when they look at the moon?
Just watch out boy, because tonight the monster isn't you.
You know what you want, but you don't know what she is.
Take my advice and give in to her kiss...

Arms go up in the air. Drinks slosh out of their plastic cups as they are raised. Half the audience starts singing along even before the chorus. Cillian, ever the showman, is reenergized as he stalks the length of the stage pouring all those long bourbon and cream sounds into the crowd below. Jack pivots, his body draped over his guitar and tuned to me even though he's blinded by the stage lights. Helene and I part. We move separately to the music, a seamless flow from shoulders to hips. I'm fucking beaming and I'm already thinking about the taste I want to give her tonight, this moment of satisfaction that I want her to feel in her mouth and in her gut.

If you're lucky, she'll give as good as she takes.
Just remember that you've always been hers to make...

Then, right in the middle of the first chorus, it's over.

"Wait, stop. Stop!" Cillian kicks the mic stand over, then turns to face the band, waving his arms at some unknown transgression. They stop one by one: first Drew, one gloved hand dropping from his stand-up bass as if he's grateful for the interruption, then Sylvy, sticks down and mouth open as he pants in a mist of his own sweat and hair.

Jack is last, guitar strings still vibrating, naked and fried notes echoing in the emptying space. After some surprised murmuring, even the audience falls silent.

"I want to try something different tonight. I want to do something special for our last song," Cillian announces once he's righted his mic stand and turned back to the audience. "We play this song every show, and I'm thinking it's time to move on." He squints into the crowd and finds me right away, where he knows I will be, in front of the merch table at the back of the room. "How about a cover? You guys like covers, right? I've got a good one, okay."

I'm frozen next to Helene, and I'm grateful she's looking at the band and not at me. They have never done this, not once in the six years I have known them.

They fucking owe me.

There is a moment of confusion as Cillian abandons the mic again and confers with the other guys. Brows knit. Heads shake. Drew shakes out his arm; I can tell his wrist is killing him. Sylvy shrugs. Jack seems to argue with Cillian, but then his shoulders drop and his fingers rake the strings, ringing out the opening chords of Concrete Blonde's "Joey".

Back in front of the mic, Cillian's body snakes to the rhythm. The crowd starts up again, the people closer to my age cheering in recognition of the song.

Cillian starts to sing. Then, just two words in, he stops short again.

"You know what? I'm tired. I'm done singing tonight. Let's make this interesting."

More confused murmuring ripples through the crowd. Someone boos. The boys keep playing behind their frontman.

"There's someone I'd like you guys to meet. Someone very special to us, who doesn't get the recognition she deserves." Cillian extends his arm, his finger slicing through the room and all the way back to where I'm standing. Every head in the place turns to me. Helene gives me both a pained and sympathetic look; she can tell I'm not in on this.

"See that gorgeous woman back there by the merch table?" Cillian continues. "That's Ronnie. Our Ronnie. She's the unsung hero of the band. She's been with us for—how long, Ronnie?—six, seven, eighteen years now, selling merch, keeping us in line, our taskmaster, our den mother. Every night she's sleeping in the van or in another shitty-ass motel room with a bunch of smelly-ass guys. She's a fucking *saint*, right? Why do you do it, Ronnie, huh? We can't fucking thank you enough."

The room swells with one giant held breath. Dozens of phones held aloft swing from the stage to me.

"Anyway, it's her turn in the spotlight. She's got some hidden talents, and it's time for everyone to see them. What do you guys think?"

The crowd roars. Every person in the place stares at me, waiting.

Cillian is grinning. "Come on, Ronnie! Get your ass up here and sing for us!"

It's a kick in the gut. He knows I can't sing. They all know that. There were plenty of nights, long drives and bored in middle-of-nowhere motel rooms, when they goaded me as I told them I couldn't. They even tried to teach me, but the pity came quicker than any results.

What really hurts, though, is I didn't expect Jack to go along with this. I look to him, but he keeps strumming, trying to bury himself beneath the steady march of the bass and drums.

"C'mon, Ronnie! Don't keep these people waiting. Get up here!"

Helene is looking at me, but I can't take my eyes off the stage. First the band can't even do the bare minimum and play my song, and now they want to humiliate me too? I shake my head and flip them off, but I'd rather be under the merch table, or, better yet, in the van driving as far away as I can from this place.

Fuck them.

I feel Helene squeeze my hand. Then she's in front of me, striding towards the stage as the crowd parts, and the phones swing in her direction, and everyone cheers.

The boys look relieved, picking up a harder rhythm once Helene hits the stage. Even Cillian keeps his mouth shut, though his grin is pinched as he hands the mic to her. Jack cuts back his guitar and starts over, the raking, ringing out opening chords of "Joey" striking through every other sound in the room.

Helene knows every word. She grips the mic with both hands and lays into it, her voice as bold and striking as Johnette Napolitano's. In her rolled-up sleeves and moto jeans she erases Cillian as he stands next to her, manages to light his face with surprise and anger and awe all at once. Her voice, every rumble and spark, blazes up through the soles of my feet, over my thighs, blooms in the center of my chest, bites into the palms of my hands. The audience is as rapt as I am. Pinned under Helene's distant gaze, I imagine myself up there with her. I imagine I'm the one singing. I imagine I'm playing guitar better than Jack ever has.

11.

I sell every remaining copy of the last album, all the bootlegs, all the stickers, and all the t-shirts except for the three extra-smalls we've been hauling around since January. Almost $800 in merch, plus the $700 guarantee: our best night in months. Helene affixes the SOLD OUT sign we rarely get to use across the band's banner while I order another batch of t-shirts to be shipped to our PO Box in New Jersey.

Then I'm done. Now I get to eat.

Not Helene, though. Even after we have no more merch to sell, people still surround the table, saucer-eyed and tipsy, effusing their admiration of Helene's performance. Will she be singing again? Does she write music? Is the band writing anything for her?

They all but say it: That voice is too good to waste behind a merch table.

While Helene alternates between demure and preening, I head out the back to the parking lot, cashbox in hand. After I stash it in the van, I survey the handful of people milling about, smoking and chatting. The night's crisp and dry, the kind of cold that feels good after steaming in the sweat of a couple hundred strangers inside a windowless brick box. The choices are better inside, but I'm willing to take someone out here if it means I can feed in a car with the windows rolled down.

I'm eyeing a woman stumbling to her car alone at the far end of the lot when I hear a familiar laugh.

Cillian pours out the club's back door with a young woman on his arm. He's playing drunk—I know that look—but under his arm the woman folds, her face split in a sloppy grin and her glassy eyes catching the moonlight. She steadies herself with a hand on his chest. Every stumble is punctuated by a giggle. As they approach the van—to feed or fuck or both—he raises that pointing finger and calls my name, drawing out a thousand *E*s that echo through the streetlight-dotted night.

"Ronnie!" Cillian exclaims again, pronouncing it normally this time. He stops short in front of me, causing the young woman to lurch forward and almost fall at my feet. He snaps her back mostly upright in his embrace. "Ronnie, beautiful, saintly Ronnie. This is my friend, uh…" He looks at the woman, but she just grins up at him. "This is my new friend… Julie? Jody?"

She giggles, then burps. "Sorry. Joanie," she says, sticking out her hand.

I take her hand in a limp shake. Her fingers are cold, and it occurs to me that she's dopey not from booze but because Cillian already had her as a snack.

"What the fuck, Cillian," I snap. "What was that in there?"

He feigns a stricken look. "Ronnie, my dear, sweet Ronnie… Whatever do you mean?"

"Don't fuck with me."

He looks at Joanie, who's now resting her head on his shoulder. Her eyes are closed, her mouth hanging open.

"You know, I'm kinda disappointed in you. I believed in you, but you sent your girlfriend up there instead. What are you so afraid of? You gotta keep practicing, girl."

"What you said. *Taskmaster*?" I say, the word even uglier on my own tongue. "Den mother?"

"They're just words. And they're not wrong. You're always keeping us in line, telling us when we can eat and when we can't. I was a good boy tonight—I waited until after we played, just like you said. We're all in this together, right? We're all equal."

"Oh, like the band? Like how you decide what they play and when?"

Cillian nudges Joanie with his chin. She snorts, but doesn't move. There's a dark circle of drool on Cillian's shoulder.

His gaze circles the parking lot before narrowing on me. "You're keeping a fucking snack in your purse while we go without."

I think of Helene back inside at the merch table, fending and feeding off compliments from all those people. People more beautiful and younger than me. Full of more life and energy and happy memories than I could ever give her.

"Oh," Cillian whistles, eyebrows hopping with his gleeful little grin. He takes an uncomfortable amount of delight in studying my face. "She's not just a snack, is she? Do you love her, or are you just fucking her? Doesn't matter. Either way, good for you. It's about time you got laid. I was worried you're turning into a dried-up old hag."

"Fuck you," I say. "Everything I do for you… Fucking washed-up rockstar wanna-be. This is the best it's ever gonna get." I gesture at the snoozing girl on his shoulder, the parking lot, the streetlight lit night sky of a middling place in a middling world. "You wouldn't be alive without me."

Cillian's talking shit again, but it doesn't matter. It doesn't matter if he goes too far yet again, if another poor fool ends up dead behind a dumpster. I'm already walking away, slicing through another throng of laughing, kissing, shouting people and back into the building.

If Jack has the keys to the van, he won't ask why I want them. If Drew or Sylvy has them, they won't care why I need them. God help me if any of them let Cillian hold onto the keys.

I just want to grab Helene, get in the van and drive. Sure, we could vanish without a word in Helene's car, but I want the boys to feel it. See what it's like without me.

Helene's got our merch display packed up, her last admirer dashing back into the crowd by the time I reach her. The headlining band—some punk/metal hybrid obsessed with murder ballads—draws most everyone to the stage, leaving the fringes we occupy empty, the air thin and cold like outside.

"Let's go. Let's get out of here," I shout.

Helene's gaze darts to the bar and the exit before circling back to me. "The guys—"

"Fuck them. You and me, let's just go."

I look down at her hand on the table, palm flat where the cash box had been. $800. The band won't get their guarantee until the end of the night, but I can let them have that—it'll assuage this ridiculous motherly guilt that's been far heavier than the endless road. The $800 I stashed in the van will get Helene and me out of here. It'll buy us a little time and a lot of space.

"You're serious."

"I'm done with them," I tell her. "Fucking Cillian, all of them. How long am I supposed to—"

"Ronnie," she cuts me off, grabbing my hand. When I tense in her grip, her fingers lace through mine and curl over my knuckles. "They're sick." She tips her head

70

towards the bar. "I tried to tell you. Drew's stomach—he's sick. Sylvy's sick. They're probably all sick."

It takes a moment, but I spot Drew sitting alone at the far end of the bar, one arm propping his head up and an untouched beer in front of him. Even from this far away he looks pale, a waxy moon of a face with two bruised hollows for eyes. He should be eating now, feasting in a corner booth, a fistful of lovelies crumpled in limp bliss in his lap. Maybe he needs antibiotics this time, but feeding should give him what he needs to get through the night. I scan the crowd, trying to spot the difference between tipsy and drained, stoned and empty. They all look like Drew could have left his mark on them. I remember the sour, musty odor that came off him in the diner; no wonder no one is sitting next to him.

And Sylvy. I don't see him anywhere. Is he backstage, unspooling a roll of paper towels around his middle? Did some poor guy or girl get some of that black ooze on their forehead and make a scene, tell their friends before Sylvy could explain? They might be sick, but we're succubi—we can go on as long as we keep feeding.

I touch my own stomach and find the comfort of soft, dry cotton.

"Their stomachs—you know what this is?" I ask Helene. "You know what's wrong with them?"

Her gaze drops down to our banner neatly folded next to the SOLD OUT sign. I untangle my hand from hers.

"Is it contagious? Just tell me," I say.

Instead of answering, she pulls me close. Her mouth finds mine, but I'm searching over her shoulder, twisting my head to catalogue every muscle-thick dude, every camera flash, any man or woman who might hurl insults or worse. The band and I have never stayed anywhere long enough to know which spaces are safe, not that that has stopped anyone but me. Though they've seen the same shit I have, Cillian especially still flaunts the recklessness of youth with no memory. Maybe they're all more alive than I'll ever be.

I twist away from Helene, but she tightens her grip on my upper arms and I give in. I close my eyes. A breath of crisp night air, the mineral bite of gin, a little brine that could be from the inside of my own mouth. Rich and round, butter and olive oil, a remedy and an indulgence. I let myself fall into her despite the prick of fear in the back of my neck. But it's not merely a kiss. She forces my mouth open and I feel that great rush of something opening up deep inside her. Her tunnel flexes and I wait for the pull— she could've asked; I would've given her whatever she needs—but instead she's pushing, *up up up* until the tunnel deep in my own core roars awake, a reflex even in those rare times when I'm not hungry. I don't have to pull. She fills my mouth and my tunnel sips until I choke.

Sunday morning bed sheets, this time knotted from sweat and restless limbs. Bare breasts loll against a heaving belly. One hand up, fingers drooping towards coils of black cord binding her wrist to the bed post. Other hand trembling atop the sheets as dark, murky liquid pours from the gaping hole where her navel used to be.

Her eyes. They're wide and dark and wet with terror. And longing. Helene, hovering over the woman, is reflected in her pupils, Helene's own body vibrating with a rush of fear and sorrow. This woman should fear her, but still, she wants Helene more than she has ever wanted anything.

I push away from Helene, hard enough that she stumbles backwards. We're in our deserted corner of the club, the headlining band is playing, no one is looking at us, but I still have one foot in the memory that she forced on me. It's fresh, an open wound she wants to cut away. No matter how much I swallow, the bitter edges of fear and regret linger on my tongue.

"That was her, your person at home," I sputter before releasing a string of coughs from deep in my chest. I spit on the floor, trying to rid my mouth of the taste. "Her stomach... like Drew and Sylvy?"

Helene rubs the back of her hand roughly over her mouth. She nods.

"And you made her one of us?"

"She begged me. After everything she gave me... I knew I shouldn't, but she wouldn't listen. I owed her."

So Helene had been weak, like me. Except my boys never asked. I just gave, as if this power, this ability, this curse was mine to give.

I gave because I was tired of being alone.

"So this thing with her stomach..." Drew's gaping wound overlaps with the memory of Helene's woman, that same purple-black ooze, a void I could slip my fingers into and feel the slick heat of intestines, the thing that feeds us and keeps us alive cleaved and seeping. "What happened to her? Where is she now?"

Her eyes drift down to the empty merch table. She doesn't say anything.

"Why didn't you tell me this sooner? You saw Drew and now Sylvy. Why didn't you tell me this would happen to them?"

"I tried."

"When?"

"In the car, yesterday, on our way to Spokane. You wouldn't listen."

I retrace every opportunity, from the car ride to the motel, to every bar and every drink last night. "Then you try again. This is too fucking important."

"I thought we had more time. I just wanted—" Her shoulders jump then deflate with her sigh. "I just wanted a perfect night with you, and I...I didn't know about the rot. I didn't know it would happen to everyone," she says. Her fingers trace the folded banner, the plastic SOLD OUT sign, the wet ring left behind by her last drink. Anything to not have to look at me. "No one talks about what happens when you make one of us because it's something we're not supposed to do. I didn't know what the fuck I was doing when I made her. I love who I am—what we are—but I felt so alone. Isn't that why you made this band? I mean, I had just made her and she got sick right away. You've been with these guys for years. So I thought they must be different, like maybe it wouldn't happen to them."

My mind catalogues all the times Drew complained of a stomachache, his arm wrapped around his belly, the nausea we all attributed to his hunger. Days, weeks, maybe even months of this; time has been a blur of lights and amps and backseats for as long as I can remember. Did he hide it because he knew it would spread, because he was afraid I or any of the other guys would drain him dry and dump him on the side of the road on our way to the next gig? How many nights did he stay awake, too afraid to ask me what was happening to him? And now Sylvy, sliding all over me, maybe even trying to give me this thing, this rot, so he won't have to suffer alone. If Cillian has it, he'd make sure we all know. If Jack has it... I haven't touched him in so long. If he's rotting too, he wouldn't let me near him.

"So, what is it exactly?" I ask. "How do we stop it?"

Helene lifts her head, her eyes flicking to the crowd in front of the stage before finally resting on me. "We can't. When they feed, they can't keep it in anymore. They can't absorb energy, memory, skill—whatever they take, it doesn't stick. I think it's because they're not real succubi, not like us. They're copies we made. Whatever they take, it burns right through them and leaks out. They're rotting."

"How long did your person have it?"

"Ronnie…"

"Fuck, Helene. Just be honest with me."

"Not long. It got worse and worse no matter what we did. I tried to keep her going, but…she was suffering."

I turn towards the bar. Drew is still there, slumped on his stool and clutching his pint glass as if it's the only thing holding him up. The band's performance drained him, burned through whatever little energy, strength and memory he was able to keep inside his gut. He's not alone now, though. A woman with long, slim braids is sitting in the seat beside him, her hand traveling up and down his arm, her face pinched with obvious concern, even from this distance. I imagine her waking up in the alley or a ride share, nearly empty, wondering how she got there and why she can't remember anything. Wondering what the foul dark substance is that coats her hands, her face, stains her clothes and makes her own stomach cramp.

"So they starve and they rot—whichever kills them first," I say.

This time Helene doesn't hesitate. Mouth a hard line, she nods, an action so slight it's like she still can't commit to the admission. I made the same mistake she did, but she could've warned me. For days now she's known what was going to happen and she let my boys and me wonder and be afraid.

I'm turning away from her when she grabs me and forces her mouth on mine again. *Up up up* she pushes into me, my hungry tunnel stronger than my will as it laps up the image of her woman's face, relief softening her eyes as Helene closes in on her. I'm filled with Helene's memory of emptying this woman, pulling from her the smell of the woman's skin, the sound of her laugher, that moment of stunned panic the first time Helene fed on her. The woman falls back into the sweaty sheets in a sort of ecstasy that I've seen before, that I don't want to remember now. Helene takes the pain in the woman's gut, the burning in her skin, the endless hollow hunger, until the woman withers under Helene's touch and—

Helene's the one to break away this time, as if the gravity of what she's forced on me finally hit her. Mouth still open, she looks horrified, a reflection of my own face.

"I'm sorry," she murmurs. Her voice is wet, clotted. "Please, Ronnie. She couldn't control herself. She was dangerous and she was suffering. I had to."

I run my palm over my mouth. My lips feel fat and raw, throbbing with blood, gums itching with a poison my body desperately wants to shed. "So that's why you're here. With me. You left her there and you ran."

"Ronnie, please…" Tears bully the edges of Helene's eyes, a shimmering weight that makes the rest of her face seem so small and so hungry. "I had to," she insists, and the tears break free in twin thin streams. "I made a mistake, and she suffered for it. I had to do it, and I wish—please, I can't live with this memory. I was supposed to keep moving, but you… I didn't expect to meet you. I followed you because—"

I turn and start walking towards the bar. "I gotta find Jack," I say.

12.

Drew's gone by the time I make it to the bar, all that's left of him and his new friend the scents of rot and hyssop lingering in the air. I follow the smell out the back exit, but don't spot any of the guys among the people smoking in the parking lot. No one's in the van, which is unlocked, though there's still a large dent in the backseat's cold vinyl bench. I check under the seat and am relieved to find the cashbox still there. It smells like weed and sweat and the icy spice of the deodorant stick the guys having been passing around since our last trip to the drug store two states ago. Only the plastic party cup on the dashboard is new.

They're feeding and fucking and I'm supposed to accept this hunger, as if it keeps me sharp, sober. The designated driver.

I save the green room for last. Even in the dives, the nowhere places, there's always some guy eager to judge and assert what little power he has. None of it ever changes.

Tonight it's a bouncer in a black STAFF t-shirt, heading away from a series of doors that flank the green room in the narrow hallway behind the stage. His eyes don't even lift from his phone as he tells me, "Bands only. Bathroom's by the bar."

"I'm with the band."

He looks up from his phone, eyes sweeping from my face to my feet and back again, a bemused grin surfacing as he squints at me standing in the spotlight of the exposed bulb overhead. "Oh, yeah? What do you play, honey?"

I picture Helene in her pointy silver-tipped boots, her narrowed eyes and bored look an implicit threat. Always worth the fight.

"I said I'm with the band. Now move, please."

The bouncer straightens, over two hundred pounds of burly hubris filling the tight space between me and door to the green room. "You know that old saying about sugar and vinegar, don't you?" he says, showing me rows of squared-off white teeth.

I could drain him, suck out all that muscle and swagger and drop him, use my new boost of strength to roll his corpse into some storage closet or back room—all these doors marked STAFF ONLY back here—where he won't be found until well after the house lights go up. Cillian would do it without even the two seconds of hesitation that holds me back now. Leave someone else to clean up.

Instead, I plant my hands on my hips and shoot the bouncer a hard stare. "Just let me in, okay?"

He laughs. "Aren't you a little too old to be a groupie?"

"Fuck off and move."

"Not with that attitude, lady," he says, smirking as he focuses on my face as if discerning my anger that seems to feed him. "Sorry, I mean *ma'am*."

Just push him against the wall. Squeeze his balls in my fist. Hold my breath and force my mouth over his, and *up up up*, take whatever I can use, even whatever nasty memories he's made over his lifetime because I can. Make sure he knows what it's like to feel small. Fucking pray he doesn't get hard.

Instead, before I can even move, I hear a voice behind me.

"C'mon, man," Jack says. "A little fucking respect, huh? She's with me."

Shrugging, the bouncer strides past us, eyes down on his phone again.

That fucking easy.

"Sorry," Jack says, his hand sliding over my arm as he moves in front of me to open the green room door. He places his hand on my shoulder as I step inside, but I shake him off. "Everyone here's a fucking asshole." He sighs. "You okay? What's up?"

We sit on a cracked leather sectional against the back wall of the small, windowless room. The table in front of us is littered with beer cans in various stages of crushed, spent matches, pizza crusts on paper plates, and a deli tray that's been picked clean except for the cauliflower. The odors of cigarette smoke, ranch dressing, and burnt plastic clot the humid air.

"Drew and Sylvy," I start, scanning the room. The bathroom door is open to reveal a pink plastic shower curtain strung between two toilets, no one in there either. Jack and I are alone. "Helene knows what's wrong with them."

Jack's features tighten. "You mean that stomach thing? Sylvy's got it too?"

"They're sick. They can't absorb what they take anymore, so they start to rot and it leaks out. That's what's happening to Drew and Sylvy, why Drew's stomach looks like that. I saw the same thing on Sylvy today. They'll rot and starve—whichever happens first."

Jack's features unclench, a dropped-bottom look hollowing out his face. "What? Are you sure? What do we do?"

"There's nothing we can do."

"That's what Helene says? How does she know?"

The bass and drums of the headlining band make the wall in front of us seem to roll in broad waves, the framed promo photos of various mid-level bands clacking against the plaster in rhythm with the music. I imagine Helene's person here, what little of her face I can picture—the woman is nothing more than a vague assemblage of the appropriate parts in the memories Helene has given me—reacting to the loud music, the screaming on the other side of the wall, every dark and dirty corner where terrible thoughts and even more terrible people might lurk. Would she worry about Helene? Would she enjoy this kind of life if Helene had given her the choice?

"She's like us—like me. She made someone like I made you guys," I say. "Except the person she made, she got sick right away. Same as what we saw with Drew. She had to…" I can't say it. Jack's not a dog I have to put down. "Come here," I say, tugging on the hem of his t-shirt.

He pushes my hand down and leans back, away from me. I watch him cross both arms over his stomach. "So she's a succubus. When were you going to tell us?" When I don't answer, he shakes his head, gives a rueful chuckle. "What are the odds, huh?"

"Jack…"

"Whatever," he says, though I know he's wounded by the secret I've kept. "That's one person. Doesn't mean it's going to happen to all of us."

"Maybe not, but it's happening to Drew and Sylvy."

"I'm fine. Cillian's fine."

I reach for him again, my fingers trailing over the dark hair dotting his arms. "Please, Jack."

With an exaggerated exhale, he unwraps his arms and allows me to lift the hem of his shirt. I lean in close under the low light. His stomach is unmarred, the trail of soft black hair running down into the top of his jeans clean and dry, his bellybutton a secretive crevice that sucks inwards with the tightening of his abdominals when my fingers venture too near. I turn on my phone's flashlight and press my finger below his navel. There's a dark red crescent in there, like the start of a bruise, but I can't tell. Maybe just a shadow.

"Told you I'm fine," Jack says, tugging his shirt back down over his belly.

I stay close, leaning over him. There's a faded smear of pale pink lipstick on his chin, barely discernible even this close up. His lips part as if to speak again, but it's a clipped intake of breath, a startled pause. A heavy bass line thuds against the opposite wall and I feel like we're hopping, Jack and I, little tics because we can't sit still.

"Let me in, okay?" I say.

Hands braced on his shoulders, I straddle him and press my mouth over his. He opens to me easily, relaxing as my tunnel stretches towards him. He doesn't push up like Helene did, but he's as wide and pliable as the drunks I've consumed, all jelly and soft like the girls on molly who were eager to give me more than just a taste.

In an open-mouthed kiss I take my time, pushing aside reserves of strength and energy, the muscle memory of his hands on his guitar, that rush he still feels from being on stage tonight. That pinch of anger he felt when Cillian tried to humiliate me. The shame he felt when he didn't stop him. Those things, I'll let him keep.

I sift through memories: when we saw Drew's stomach at the diner, fresh in Jack's mind after I told him about the rot; how soft my lips were against his calloused fingers when he held the joint to my mouth; Helene sweeping me into our motel room as I blew him a kiss. Now I feel the sting, and I don't want any of it.

Fresher memories come up next: a woman with bleached, close-cropped hair smiling at him at the bar; Cillian walking by with Joanie on his arm; Cillian again with another woman sporting huge golden dagger earrings, asking Jack if he wanted a little while the woman, tipsy, giggled uncomfortably; walking in on Drew in the bathroom going down on a guy with spiky black hair; Sylvy blowing a guy wearing thick silver rings on every finger in the green room; Drew again, this time in the parking lot kissing a leathery woman with only one shoe as she slumped against the van. Jack's own thoughts mirror mine in each moment: *I have never seen them this fucking greedy. Ravenous.*

A flash of him sitting in the van—today? last night? last week? I can't tell—as a hot needle slowly hollowed out his guts, fear keeping his fingers away even as he knew he needed to lift up his shirt and look—

Jack pulls me out. He's still open, but I can't concentrate, can't find what I'm looking for because now his hands are up under my jaw, fingers entwined in the hair at my temples, his tongue pushing into my mouth in a hunger that doesn't feel like a distraction. He tastes of the warm spice of whisky and something else, something I can't quite place, this film of sweetness that makes my teeth itch. His fingers crawl around to the back of my head, pulling me even closer so that every inch of our exposed skin is pressed together, as if he might at any moment flip this around, unclench his own tunnel and try to suck everything I have into him. But he doesn't. He stays pliant and open, and I'm in that bathtub again, knees aching, my core filling up with whatever I could take like the last time he fed me.

So I take a little off the top: the beautiful young woman who came into the green room—she flashed a gap-toothed smile and the same bouncer who treated me like shit waved her right in—and told him how amazing the band was tonight, the chain strap of her purse rattling while her hand roamed over his thigh; the woman with the bleached cropped hair he first saw at the bar, now in the van with him, slowly going slack beneath his body; a wiry young man in the club's back office, only the desk holding him up as Jack worked between his legs. I've never seen Jack feed on this many people in one night.

When I attempt to dig deeper, Jack begins to close himself off. It's so easy to fall into him. There's comfort in being held by him, of being wanted, of not having to work for his loyalty or his heart. I've had sex with Jack before—actual sex, not just for feeding—and I enjoyed it. We were bored, lonely, somewhere outside Omaha. He's a good kisser, and his touch had felt just as satisfying as it does now. Even then, I wanted so badly to feel the same about him as he does about me, but I just…didn't. It never felt right to me, not enough for the kind of love he wants.

His hands drift down to my ass and I think of Helene again, the magnet of her brazen stare the first time I saw her, the sound of my name in her mouth, her electric lines that bolted right into me the moment we touched. How she can open me up whenever she wants. How—even now, when I'm angry at her—I want her to.

"We can't…" I start, breaking away from Jack.

He nods, rubs the side of his hand over his bottom lip. Dusky pink and glistening from my lipstick all over his mouth. "You're in love with her."

I don't know if I love her. I don't know if I'm in love. It's been so long since I experienced love without the weight of responsibility and need that maybe I can't recognize anything else.

"I barely know her," I say.

His hands slide from my ass down to his sides. I ease off his lap, the leather cushions heaving a rustling sigh beneath me. Jack concentrates on fixing his t-shirt, smoothing it over the top of his jeans.

I scoot over, ready to stand and walk out and give him some privacy, when my hand catches on something small and cold and hard on the couch. It pools towards my touch.

Metal. A row of little silver links, the chain strap of a slick black purse trapped between the cushion and the back of the couch.

I look at Jack, but he won't look at me. I squint in the low-lit room. An oversized gold dagger earring winks between crushed cans on the coffee table. A blocky silver ring rests next to a broccoli floret smashed into the thin carpet at my feet. My gaze catches on a woman's studded flat peeking out from between two battered guitar cases across the room.

People lose jewelry all the time, often not noticing until they get home. A purse and a shoe, though, you would know. You wouldn't leave without trying to find them.

Jack finally turns to me and gives me that look, that *here's another gin and tonic because things are about to go wrong* look. On the other side of the wall, the headlining band drones on, an endless whirl of bass and drums and a screeching guitar solo that makes this night longer than it needs to be. They're loud, and I've damaged my hearing over the years, but the band's not loud enough to block out the voices. Though dulled by distance and drywall, the voices are becoming distinct, rising. Not words yet, but sounds. Terrible sounds.

Down the hall, behind the stage, someone, then everyone, starts screaming.

13.

This is how it is when you drain someone:

They don't succumb to the ecstasy. At first, it's whatever ambivalence one feels during a sloppy backseat/alley/bathroom tryst. There's the moment when it turns, though, when your sipping becomes thirsty gulp after gulp as your tunnel roars all the way open and you can't control yourself anymore. They struggle, of course, your prey, when they realize this kiss or fuck is not what they thought, that you are some different kind of creature—they never think you're a succubus; they don't know that word—who is turning them inside out, sucking every ounce of strength they have into you. Regret and fear tussle, thoughts racing as fast as their fingers clawing and legs kicking. The fight deflates quickly, though, because every succubus knows you take the muscle, the brawn, the energy first. Your prey gives in and then you can start to take their skills. Their memories.

You empty those thoughts. You consume every memory until they have nothing left to fight for. You snatch talent and skill from the front of the brain all the way down to deep in the muscle. You make it yours, tuck it away in your DNA, or let it wither and die from disuse. Whether you want it or not—if you are a smart succubus—you take it all.

As you feed, the body beneath/against/atop yours deflates. Muscles atrophy, detaching and drooping, pooling into the soft fat that now loosens over brittle armature. Skin slackens. Wizens. An inverse suction like vacuum-sealing. You actually hear a rattle as you suck your prey hollow, a clack of featherweight bone against bone in your grip. They age forty, fifty, sixty—whatever they had left—years, saggy lines and burst purple veins all that's left of once plump flesh, only recognizable by the clothes they are wearing. Their makeup. Their jewelry. Their eyes now bulging in a sunken face, pupils still huge and shiny and black with fear.

A husk. Like the birthday guy we found behind the dumpster just a few nights ago, when I first met Helene. I've never drained a person, but I remember every rabbit, how all that was left looked like dried-out roadkill. Just a ragged pelt and a few bones I couldn't even name.

I turn to Jack next to me, but he's still staring at the pile of bodies: Joanie, Cillian's dagger-earring woman, Drew's spiky-haired man, Sylvy's guy with the silver rings, Drew's parking lot paramour, Jack's woman with the bleached cropped hair, the woman with the chain-strap purse, Drew's friend with the braids. They all lay in a sloppy heap filling the narrow hallway behind the stage, bodies poured out of the storage closet three doors down from the green room, a heart attack for the poor staff member who just wanted a roll of paper towels or a case of plastic cups.

The screaming has stopped, but it starts again with every new person who crowds into the hallway to see what all the commotion is about. Even the headlining band is here, middle-aged guys with the same frizzy long black hair, all crowded in the doorway that leads from the stage. They're closest to Jack and me; we're trapped with only the green room behind us. A murmur ripples through the crowd on the other side of the bodies. Phones come out. Someone calls 911. Everyone else is shooting video, taking photos, an unending string of flashes blinding my peripheral vision. The narrow space fills with sweat, beer-breath, and the sweet licorice scent of hyssop, a soft warm cloud over the cooling bodies.

A young woman steps forward and crouches down, pulling an arm out of the pile. The guy with the silver rings. She presses two fingers to his wrist, then moves on to the other bodies. She checks crepe-y necks and sagging jaw lines for a pulse. The crowd chatters, heads shake. Someone does a poor job of suppressing a snicker. No one recognizes their friends, not yet. All these people see are old rock sluts, their slack mouths and wrinkled foreheads smeared with an oily black substance.

"Grandma shoulda stayed home," some dick with a shaved head whoops.

Jack's hand brushes mine and he gives me an oddly hopeful look. *Maybe everyone will think they all died of heart attacks*.

These bodies are hollow, though. Brittle. Every time the woman checking for pulses touches another one, I'm terrified her fingers will burst right through papery flesh, straight to bone.

And we have no way out.

Between phone camera flashes, I squint into the crowd, though I can't see all the people who are around the bend of the hallway, still pushing in to get a glimpse of the carnage. Cillian stands out because of his black quiff, lazy arm around a slack-jawed young man as he casually surveys what he's done. Sylvy catches my eye right away because he's one of a handful of people who are moving backwards through the crowd towards the main floor and presumably the exit. I don't see Drew anywhere. I don't see Helene.

"They're dead. They're all dead," the woman who was checking pulses says. Her voice is flat, strangely empty for that kind of announcement.

With a string of *ohmygodohmygodohmygod*, the frenzy starts up again, a whirl of bodies turning and flailing like in the pit, but this time the only music is a chorus of screams. Phones are still held aloft and filming even as people race back out onto the club's floor, arms pushing and feet tripping, putting as much distance as they can between themselves and the drained dead. I want to look for Helene, but Jack grabs my hand and we're running with the crowd. Past the stage, past the merch table with our banner and SOLD OUT sign still sitting there, out into the cold night air. We look as innocent and scared as everyone else.

Except they saw, didn't they? There are too many people here, the club so full throughout the night that there's no way Cillian, Drew, Sylvy and Jack fed unseen. The people in the parking lot stare as they rush to their cars, eyes catching on Jack and me because we don't look scared enough, because our fear looks different. Someone saw Cillian with way too many people tonight. Someone noticed the people who slipped away with Drew and never came back. Several someones are realizing that their friends are missing. At least one person will look at the video they shot and notice the dagger earring, the braids, the silver rings and realize these poor dead old people stuffed in that closet are familiar. People they know. People who walked into the club young and never came back out.

The air outside smells like fertilizer and something burnt, like a snuffed-out match; it travels in thick ropes up my nostrils, making my sinuses ache. Jack laments his guitar left behind in the green room and I want to corner the people who stare at us, but he doesn't let either of us make those mistakes. There are too many people to drain of their memories of tonight, and the photos and videos have propagated beyond our control by now. Though we didn't feed tonight, Helene and I are not safe. People saw me with the band. They saw Helene singing on stage.

We're fucked.

All we can do is get in the van.

14.

We find Drew and Sylvy two blocks from the club, sitting on a curb in front of a closed auto shop. Drew's white t-shirt is covered in dark liquid from collar to hem, more of the same foul fluid a faded smear around his mouth. Sylvy has to help him stand. As he eases Drew inside, the sour odor of damp, wizened skin fills the van.

Cillian texts us while we're grabbing our stuff at the motel. He's with a new friend in a mid-90s blue Plymouth. He wants us to follow them to Idaho.

This is my chance to say what we're all thinking: *Fuck Cillian, he's gonna get us killed, let's head back west.* Except, once we're back in the van, Sylvy's in the way backseat cradling a barely-conscious Drew in his lap, and Jack's already getting on 195 South. It's in our bones to never leave family behind, no matter what they do.

And now they've all done the same shit Cillian did.

We catch up to the blue Plymouth pretty quickly; Cillian waves out the window as confirmation. None of us talk in the van, so I try to focus on the sound of Drew's rattling breath. We should be making a plan, something better than Cillian's let's-go-to-a-stranger's house solution, but we're all too tired. The panic adrenaline wore off after our stop at the motel. With every car that passes us, I wonder if they were at the club too, if they recognize me or Jack, if the image of Sylvy draining a guy dead in the bathroom is burned into their memory. Who saw us get in the van? Did they memorize the license plate? Though we've been in similar situations and gotten away, I can't be sure the lack of sirens means we'll be as lucky this time. It's never been as bad as tonight.

It's almost worse thinking about Helene. I worry about where she might be, if she made it out of the club, if she even knows that I grabbed her stuff too while I was at the motel. I keep imagining her heading back to her dead woman at home, or starting over somewhere else, all those miles putting enough distance between us so that I can be nothing more than a question mark in her memory. A hallucination, a dream? A drinking binge that spawned a string of poor decisions? I'll be a story she tells her grandkids one day, if she even remembers my name at all. All while I sit in another dingy motel room in another shitty town holding one of her shirts against my face as I try to suck the last of her faded juniper and musk into my mouth.

Then she texts: *Where are you? Are you okay?*

It's been at least twenty minutes since we left the motel. Why did she wait this long? With what happened at the club... Did she even think of me?

No, what happened was a I met a woman and we had some fun, and I'm the one who fucked it up by making it into something it isn't. She had a little adventure and I got attached. Why did I even think I could tell her all those things, things about myself and the band that now—especially now—could get us detained and killed? I should know better, after all these years on the road. Really, I just hate myself.

My phone buzzes again. *Ronnie. Please. Just tell me you're okay.*

All my Ns warm cream rolling off her tongue. Her hand warm and firm on my stomach. That perfect shape where she fits. Where I fit.

I text Cillian for our destination then text the address to Helene.

92

15.

Almost two hours later, we arrive in a tidy suburban neighborhood in Moscow, Idaho. Jack maneuvers the van into the narrow driveway of a pale yellow rambler, right behind the Plymouth. The night is silent, not even leaves rustling in the breeze, and barely a hint of tires on the main road two blocks away. We're silent too as we get out of the van, Jack and Sylvy propping a delirious Drew between them. I scan the neighboring houses and see nothing but rows of closed curtains and the glowing yellow dots of porch bulbs, the markers of what I hope is a sound sleep for every occupant. Only the yellow rambler's windows are uncovered, revealing Cillian and his new friend lit up in the living room as they sit close on the couch, beer bottles in hand.

I lead the way up the path and hold open the unlocked front door for Jack, Sylvy and Drew. Only Cillian's friend rises to help.

"Oh, shit," he says, sweeping us into the house. He's young, handsome, with a square jaw on a round face. Drew lifts his head, and a thin stream of black liquid trickles from the corner of his open mouth.

Cillian raises his beer. "Everyone, this is Conor. Conor, everyone." Conor shuts the door and Cillian squints out the window, though I can't discern much beyond pinpricks of porch and streetlights and our own reflections staring back at us. "Well, not everyone, I guess," he adds, shooting me a wry little grin. "Where's your girlfriend, Ronnie?"

Same as he feeds on people, Cillian also feeds on indignity. I already gave him what he wanted outside the club, when he introduced me to one of his many snacks of the night, Joanie; I'm not doing it again. When I reach over him to shut the curtains, he utters a mealy little "rude", but doesn't push any further.

"Does he need to go to the ER?" Conor asks, uneasy eyes on Drew still draped between Jack and Sylvy.

"No hospitals," both guys say at once.

Conor leads us down the hall to a small bedroom with a bed in the center and a small desk in the corner. Two of the band's early vinyl album covers are pinned to the wall. The guys brood down at me from the cover of their debut, the four of them gathered under a lone streetlight, cartoon flames encircling them as they try their hardest to look like they'd rather be anywhere else. We hadn't even met yet, back when they still pretended to be jaded.

After we get Drew settled in the bed, Conor leaves to rejoin Cillian in the living room. He's left us some towels, water, and hydrogen peroxide, but I can barely peel Drew's shirt from his stomach. The flow of blood and liquid rot that leaked from his abdomen has mostly subsided, leaving a thick crust that's merged his skin with the cotton of his shirt. We're all afraid to cause him more pain, even though his only sign of consciousness is the occasional phlegmy moan as Jack, Sylvy and I stand over him, rigid with worry.

"I could feed him," I say more to myself than the boys, "but I don't think that will do much."

"Water through a sieve," Jack says.

"What do we do?" Sylvy asks.

I search the memories Helene gave me of her woman. That last image of when she was tied to the bed, delirious and desperate, leaking purple-black rot all over the sheets—that had to have been the end, right before Helene killed her. The memories she gave me from before, warm

94

sheets and steam and the haze of infatuation—had she made the woman a succubus yet? Helene said she got sick right after she made her. Still, there had to be stages between that first burst of new life and the woman's guts spilled on the sheets as she begged for mercy. At what point did she look like Drew does now? I know, but I don't even want to say it inside my mind.

"How are you, Sylvy?" I nod his way. His shirt looks clean, dry.

His arms creep over his stomach and he straightens. "I'm fine."

Jack and I exchange a look.

What the fuck are we doing here? Barely two hours from the slaughter the band made, something we can't outrun this time, not with that many witnesses. Drew, and maybe Sylvy too, will die in a stranger's house in Idaho, and Jack, Cillian and I will either kill each other or end up in prison.

Laughter drifts from down the hall. The clinking of bottles, as if this is the after party, nothing more than a casual hookup before another early morning on the road.

"We're not staying," Jack says, though his tone isn't definitive. "We don't know who the fuck this guy is or what Cillian's told him."

Sylvy's gaze lingers on Drew. Despite his posturing, his worry is thick and heavy in the small room. "We have to get him help. Ronnie, where do we go?"

When I don't answer, Jack pulls out his phone and searches the club's name, then the band's name. No hits on any news sites, but when he clicks the YouTube link, we crowd around him to watch.

The band on stage, the chatter of the crowd making a muddled miasma of the guitar and vocals. Helene performing "Joey", the camera zoomed in from a distance. Drew in the crowd, notable because of the black stain on his shirt and around his mouth. Blurs of people running through the club, screaming. Close-ups of wizened arms and legs and faces, that pile of the drained-dead behind the stage. There are already six videos up, all with titles like "Rock Show Deaths" and "Spokane Club Massacre". It doesn't matter that the boys aren't recognizable in the grainy cell phone footage. The band's name is listed in the comments. They'll never play again.

"Fuck," Sylvy breathes.

Jack pauses the video and slips his phone back into his pocket. "We'll take some time. Hide out for a couple of months. Some middle of nowhere place. Somewhere cheap."

"You did this to yourselves," I say.

Sylvy shoots me a wounded look. Jack looks down at Drew. Drew rolls his sweaty head on the pillow and releases a soft groan.

"I saw you," I tell them. "Every one of you. You were so fucking greedy with all those people around. You know better. We eat when we need to and we don't kill unless we have to." Sylvy opens his mouth, but I keep going. "But no, you think you can do whatever the fuck you want now and somehow it's all going to be okay, like I'm going to take care of you and fix whatever you fuck up. What did you think was going to happen? How could you be so reckless?"

Jack runs a hand roughly over his face. He still won't look at me. "Drew's not well, Ronnie, and Cillian—"

"It's not just him," I say sharply, and Jack's body stiffens against the reminder. Was there ever a moment when he was draining the woman in the green room, or the blonde in the van, or the young man in the club's back office, that he knew he'd gotten enough, that he should stop? Even on the days we hadn't eaten, when those hours stretched into unbearable torture and we were the most desperate we'd ever been, Jack especially had always been able to control himself, even without the weight of my eye on him. I remember that dark shadow in his bellybutton, but I tell myself it's nothing; I'd rather believe he was caught up in the moment, driven by alcohol and greed like Cillian.

"You were all careless," I continue. "If you're pissed at me, fine, but this is how you act out? It's over now! We have nothing!"

No one says anything for a long time. It makes me angry to think that they're just waiting for me to get it all out, to tire myself out, but neither Jack nor Sylvy smirks like Cillian would. There are no snappy little comebacks, no belittling words, no hysteric bitch jokes. The thing is, I know how to handle Cillian. I know when I'm feeding his hunger for conflict and when his lashing out means I'm actually getting through to him. With Jack and Sylvy, I feel cruel, as if I've kicked a puppy for doing what comes naturally to him.

"You're right, Ronnie," Jack finally says. He keeps his eyes on Drew, his body deflating around a framework that won't allow him the mercy of collapse. "We just… There's no excuse. We fucked up. Our shit's still there. My guitar, Drew's bass… God, we didn't even get our guarantee."

"We made $800 on merch. It's in the van," I say.

"That's not even enough to get us across the country. We need to get *out* of the country."

Sylvy's arms are wrapped around his middle and he looks like he's going to vomit. When he turns to me I can see how scared he is, and I'm their mother all over again. "Ronnie, what do we do?"

"I don't fucking know."

All I know is that this was going to happen eventually, even if this sickness didn't exist, even if they weren't greedy assholes, even if I'd let them eat instead of insisting on a misguided measure of control. I can't even blame Cillian anymore. One or all of us, we were bound to go too far, and we are due to run out of luck. If our paths hadn't crossed, they would be just another traveling band. Jack, Drew, Sylvy, Cillian—they wouldn't be murderers. Maybe they'd have families and homes. They wouldn't have to keep moving. So it is my fault. I'm responsible for them. I made this band succubi like me because I was selfish and lonely, and now I'm finally getting my punishment. I'll have to watch what I made—my family—wither and die.

16.

We come to an agreement: get some rest here at Conor's house, check the news, stop looking at the club massacre videos, fill up the van and head east tomorrow night. Keep moving until the money runs out. And when the money runs out... we'll deal with that later.

No one says it, but we all know it: we don't leave Drew behind. He may be safer here, but there's no way he'd want to die alone in a stranger's bed, and there's no way we'd let him. I'm already picturing him slipping away in some cheap motel room in the middle of nowhere, but he will be surrounded by his family. He will die in my arms.

Sylvy's already talking about reinvention because he's drunk. Conor puts out a case of PBR, a fifth of bourbon, and a variety of pipes, vapes, and weed, and it's all claimed in seconds, as if that's all we needed to fix this night. Sylvy's already got a new band name and he goads Jack about all those new songs Jack's been writing, how they've had enough material for a new album for years, so why not now? They can tweak those songs, play a little different, sing a little different. Cut and dye their hair, turn the next feed into a feast so they can look ten years younger.

Everyone looks at Conor, the meal that will get us to our next stop.

Cillian hooks his arm around Conor and pulls him close. I didn't notice Conor at the Spokane show and I never saw him in the memories I took from Jack, so I'm not sure how long Cillian has been with him. He would've fed off him by now, taken at least a little strength and energy before the rest of us got here. Conor's not sloppy enough to have lost much, not yet anyway. He knows about what happened at the club—Cillian didn't take that—and he doesn't seem afraid of us. The way he nuzzles Cillian, it's clear he believes he's providing more than a snack and a warm bed.

As Sylvy goes on and on about the new band and Cillian joins in and Conor nods excitedly, Jack doesn't say a word. He sits in the armchair, long legs crossed in front of him, sipping on the bottle of bourbon. It's the cheap stuff, cloyingly sweet and lacking the sharp spices that would give us the heat we're seeking. He passes the bottle to me and a wave of brown sugar and vanilla rises between us. This is the best we can hope for, isn't it? We—this band—are nothing without our past. We've lost our established fan base and will have to start over, working our way up from the dank backwoods dives that'll have us, paid in nothing more than free well drinks and rounds of pool. No t-shirts, no bootlegs, no money to record an album. We'll live in that fucking van until the wheels fall off.

I'd be better off leaving now. Take the $800 from the cashbox, give myself a good head start and head east while the boys are asleep, feed enough so that I look twenty years younger, then hitch myself to whatever band needs a merch girl. Honey, baby, sweetheart, *no groupies beyond this point, ma'am.* I'll give them a little taste if I have to, but I'll never again let my loneliness lead me to the same mistakes.

I'll do what Helene did, what she's doing right now. Tomorrow night she'll be at a bar in Vancouver, sending out that intoxicating, unwavering fuck-stare to another fool with no anchor and an empty bed.

Then, just when I'm thinking about that little mountain town outside Denver, there's a knock at the door.

We all stop talking and look at each other. The cops wouldn't have figured it out by now, right? Could it be a nosy neighbor wondering about the lights and noise coming from the house at three in the morning? Conor doesn't rise until Cillian nods.

It's Helene.

She enters the house after a moment of hesitation and waits for an invitation before grabbing a beer and sitting down in the chair next to mine. She looks small, tired, a little rattled. Her forehead is greasy, and she brings with her the odors of stale beer and french fries, cigarette smoke in her hair. She looks at me as if for a sign, an all-is-forgiven. I want to touch her, feel some proof that those hands are the same ones that held me close less than twenty-four hours ago, that mouth the same one I—stupidly, deludedly—thought I knew so well.

"How's Drew?" she asks after she and Conor make their introductions.

"Sleeping," Jack says. *Dying*, I think. Jack pulls out his phone. "You seen the videos yet?"

While Jack shows Helene all of the cleverly-titled videos from the club, Cillian scoots across the couch and leans close to me. "Good for you, Ronnie," he whispers with a wink. "Looks like you managed to snag a keeper."

"Like Conor here?" I ask.

Cillian shrugs. "Us and our snacks."

"What does he know? What did you promise him?"

"Nothing more than ecstasy, momma bear."

It's not just the weed that dulls me in this moment; I don't have enough energy left for anger, for anything Cillian deserves. Just like when he scratched me then cried in my arms on the night I made him, deep down he's still that same scared little boy who believes in a parent's love.

"He knows too much, and he can't come with us," I say, careful to keep my voice down. I turn an eye to Conor, but he's talking to Sylvy now, a springboard for various new band names. "One of us is going to have to take all his memories of the last twenty-four hours. I'm not going to let you kill him."

Grinning a heady little grin, Cillian reaches out and squeezes my hand. When I pull away, he shakes his head.

"You're gonna love him, Ronnie. He's delicious. His memories are so, so sweet, all these hugs from mom and dad, and trips to the county fair, blue ribbons and band camp, like a happy childhood. I would never deny you that, you know."

I turn to Helene. She looks like Jack now. He's put his phone away and they're both leaned back in their seats, a cloud of smoke between them, bottles raised to their lips, staring right through the wall.

"I need to talk to you," I tell her.

I lead Helene down the hall to the bathroom. Before I can even shut the door, she's got me pressed up against the sink, her arms draped over my shoulders, her eyes wet and dopey as she goes in for a kiss. When I push her away, she crumples against the door, shutting it.

"Where have you been?" I ask. "Why did you come here?"

"You gave me the address," she says, sniffling. She pulls her sleeve over her hand and wipes it roughly over her nose and mouth.

"I didn't see you at the motel. I got your stuff."

"I don't care about my stuff."

"Then why are you here?"

At this she raises her head and gives me a hard stare. Her eyes are huge from this angle, deep brown and heavily ringed in smeared eyeliner and exhaustion. I won't give in; I want to hear her say it.

"Why do you think? I wanted to make sure you're okay."

"You should take off in the morning," I tell her. "Put some distance between us while you can."

Helene's laugh is rueful, the kind that makes her chest hitch. "I just saw the video, Ronnie. It's too late."

"The quality's shitty. You haven't been traveling with us long. No one knows your name. They can't identify you."

"I started to drive," she says, rising. She wipes her sleeve across her eyes this time, smearing more eyeliner over raw, red skin. "I thought I'd head down to Portland, make my way through northern California."

I picture her in her unassuming black sedan, wandering the edges of backwoods towns and mid-sized cities, with her pointy-boot swagger and silver tongue, unable to blend in even if she tried. All I can offer her is a ranking of the motels along the way.

"But I don't have anywhere to go," she continues. "I don't mind traveling; I don't mind not having a destination—I just want to do it with you."

I roll my eyes. "Don't tell me you came back for me."

"God, would you stop it? Why can't you believe that? That night I first saw you... I should be halfway across the country by now."

"How long do you plan on following us?"

Helene pushes off the door and plants herself in front of me, trapping me against the sink again. I look to the side, down at the toilet with its fuzzy pink lid cover, all pilled and faded like a remnant from a grandmother's house. When her hands find my upper arms, I get a whiff under the smoke and fast food: the tang of restlessness and hunger, of my own kind.

"Don't act like this, Ronnie," she says, pulling back. "We could do this, just you and me. We can go anywhere we want."

What I want is to kiss her. I want to taste the only person who's ever felt familiar and right, DNA that is not mine but knows me. "You know I can't do that."

"You want to."

"Look what happened. I can't leave them alone. I owe them. They need me."

"They're going to get you killed."

She's right, but how many times have I been so hungry, so desperate that I got sloppy, took too much, or left my prey with a vague image of my face or name when I was too rushed to dig deep enough? How many times was my hunger so ferocious that I left someone drained of everything but their first name? It doesn't matter that they're grown men; I broke the rules and made these creatures. I'll be paying this debt until I die. Until they die.

Music rises in the living room, the band's second album, the one with my song. Helene starts to sway her hips, then her shoulders in front of me. Her hands find my waist and she presses into me, tucking her head into my neck. Her breath is so warm, the brush of her lips against my skin sending bright, hot bolts across my chest. My anger at what she kept from me—or what I didn't want to hear—is still there, but I'm so tired, and she feels so good, and she could've been in Oregon or Canada by now but she chose to ruin her life here in Idaho with me. Though there's nothing soft or romantic in the sound of Cillian wailing about being turned into a succubus, I wrap my arms around Helene and we gently sway.

"I love you, Ronnie," she whispers against my throat. "There's no one else like us, and we found each other. We're so fucking powerful when we're together."

I undo the button of her jeans and slip my hand inside. She leans into my movements, face smashed into my throat then moving upwards until she finds my mouth. The moment our lips meet, I feel her open up deep in her core, already pushing up and into me before my tunnel starts reaching. The hunger is heavy-bottomed, a flood of heat in my pelvis, an ache that fills from my gut to my knees. Her scent is thick in my nostrils, salty and sweet on my lips.

You know what you want, but you don't know what she is. Take my advice and give in to her kiss...

The music coming from the living room turns vicious, aggressive, powering the movement of my fingers hooked inside her. She kisses just as viciously. Our mouths locked together, her tunnel pushes into mine, giving faster than I can take, and I sort through what she offers: strength, confidence, a lingering taste of youth, memories of lazy Sunday breakfasts and clean sheets and fitting herself into a space that never felt right with a person who never was right.

As she comes, I take one thing from her: her last memory of her person at home, the woman's necrotizing guts steaming in the open air, her fear and relief as Helene drains her, then the moment of strange ecstasy as the last of her slips away in Helene's mouth, in Helene's embrace.

17.

Over the last six years with the band, I've managed to make myself comfortable in all sorts of strange places: the backseat of the van, wedged between Drew's bass and Sylvy snoring on my shoulder; on skanky green room couches where the odors of spilled beer and farts clung to my hair for days; in the back rows of movie theaters where catching a quick nap is cheaper than renting a room. For the overnights, the rule's always been that I sleep alone, but that just means I don't share a bed. I've crashed on strangers' floors, the boys a fort of musk and pizza breath around me. I've dozed in hotel lobbies, in hospital waiting rooms, in Cillian's lap while the vomit from the last person he fed on crusts on his shirt. The last six years of my life could be chronicled in unpleasant smells, but there's one odor I will never get used to.

Rot. The fetid odor of what should be inside creeping out and decomposing in the open air.

Drew is dying six feet away from me—how could I sleep? Helene turns over in the nest of blankets Conor made for us on the floor, scratching her face, burying her nose in her pillow, turning to the wall then the grimy carpet as if that could tame the hot blanket of death coming down on us from across the room. I'd open a window, but Drew is shivering, and I'm afraid to move the curtains, afraid someone might see my face in the brief moment it will take me to lift the sash.

Is there really nothing we can do for him? Helene has only seen this kind of suffering and decay once, and the only answer she found was to quicken the inevitable death. There's no special network, no handbook, no way that I know of to find others like us. Even if there was, I'm not sure either Helene or I would be willing to admit the wrong we did, how we got here.

I'm more comfortable perched on the edge of Drew's bed, my hand anxiously fluttering over the damp, waxy planes of his face. He seems to sleep, the raspy stutter of his breath the only indication that he's still alive. When I made him, he took what I gave and fell asleep right away. At that time, I had no idea what he would do when he awoke, but in those few hours, in a motel room in central California, I watched him in quiet awe, as if he were my newborn child.

I change his towels, dab hydrogen peroxide along the gaping chasm of his split-open stomach, push everything back in as gently as I can, until he moans in pain. I feel a pang of guilt for the mess he's made of Conor's sheets, then scold myself for the ridiculous thought. Drew's organs are indiscernible, dark gelatinous shapes bleeding into each other, shifting as his intestines unravel in a slow ooze. I gag, and the guilt there is sturdy, deserved. Even if we didn't have to answer questions, even if we had the money for the best surgeons in the world, we wouldn't be able to save him.

Will he beg me for mercy the same way Helene's woman did?

Maybe it would be better for Drew to die here, in the comfort of a kind stranger's bed. I think about getting Jack and Sylvy from the where they're sleeping in the living room, and Cillian from Conor's bed. We'll tell him we love him and each take the pain from him until there is nothing left. He'll die in a strange place, but it will be better than being on the road, left behind for a motel housekeeper to find days later, just a ragged pelt and bones you can't even name.

Then Sylvy will see what it's like. He'll be prepared when his time comes.

"I can do it," Helene says, coming up beside me. She places a hand on my shoulder and squeezes.

"No," I say.

She lowers herself next to me. Her fingers outline Drew's hand atop the blanket. Black and red liquid inches towards her, but she doesn't move. "I mean I can feed him. Get him mobile at least, so we can get out of here."

Drew inhales sharply, causing a thin stream of fluid to gush over the jumble of his insides, onto his thigh and through the towels I've arranged around him. It's so much worse, of course, but it helps me to think of it as wasted food, a dribble of vomit. In the miasma of bruised black and tepid blood that gurgles from his ruptured tunnel, I imagine the woman with the braids, the guy with the spiky black hair, the woman with one shoe—everyone he fed on at the show, all of their strength and health and memories leaking out, undigested.

"You and I both know that won't do any good," I tell Helene.

"Then we'll take his pain."

I remember what she said to me right before we left for Spokane. "That's like eating poison," I remind her. When she doesn't respond, I say, "Did it hurt? Did you get sick after you drained your person?"

She rakes her fingers between Drew's, clutching his limp hand briefly. He's tissue paper over bones, and she's plush and slick and strong. A home at any point on an endless road. "It's the way it should be," she answers.

"Even if we made a mistake, we still love them. The pain makes it real."

I'm headed to wake the boys, tell them what's going to happen to Drew and what we need to do, when Conor stumbles out in front of me in the hall. I'm almost glad to see him; I wouldn't have been surprised if Cillian had already drained him, stuffed his body in a closet, and declared ownership of this house.

"Hey, Ronnie, I need to talk to you," he says, the top half of his body swinging uncomfortably close to me. He steadies himself against the wall. His eyes are bloodshot and a thin sheen of perspiration coats his face.

"Yeah?"

His head nods forward and he struggles to catch himself, adding his shoulder to his palm braced against the wall. "You like it here, right? I'm a good host?"

"Sure. We'll be out of your hair in a few hours, okay?"

"No, no, no…" Conor straightens, his dopey grin wavering. "You don't have to go. I love this band. I drove all the way to Spokane to see you guys. I'm a true fan. And then I got to meet you tonight. I got to meet Cillian." He hiccups, looks like he might vomit, then swallows before continuing. To anyone else he appears drunk, but instead of alcohol I smell Cillian all over him. "I'm happy to do anything you guys need. You have to know that okay? I'll hide you, I'll keep you safe. It's just that Cillian said… he promised and now he says he can't."

As Conor sways in front of me, I struggle to peer over his shoulder into the living room. Sylvy's a dark shape on the couch, face down with a mess of hair and one arm grazing the floor. Jack's in the armchair, chin to chest; he'll hurt when the sun comes up. Time is running out and I want us—my family—all together with Drew, but Conor keeps babbling about some promise from Cillian, and it's not my damn fault this kid was too dumb to notice we don't have rock star money, certainly not after last night and—

"I'm one of you, Ronnie. I'm a succubus too."

Wait. How does he even know we exist? If he saw something, why didn't Cillian take the memory from him? *Not fucking possible.*

"Okay, like, not *literally*, but in my heart," Conor clarifies. "I'm meant to be one of you. I would do anything for you guys, but this is dangerous shit. People died last night. I'm taking a big risk letting you stay here. Cillian sees it in me, and he said you owe me. He said he'd make me one of you."

"You're drunk," I say, attempting to push past him. "Whatever he told you, he's just having some fun. He's fucking with you."

Conor throws both arms out, trapping me in the hall. "But he can't do it, can he? He said he would, but then he told me about you. You have to do it. You have to make me a succubus like you. Like them."

Fucking Cillian. I say it a million times a day, but he's never done anything like this before. Whether it was in a fit of desire or anger, he broke our code—the one thing we all agreed to, the one thing that keeps our family safe—which is even worse than what he did to those people at the club last night. We are at our most vulnerable, and this kind of pettiness is enough to unravel the last six years. He betrayed his brothers. He betrayed me.

"I don't know what you're talking about," I say, ducking to slip under Conor's outstretched arm.

He bumps his hip into the wall, then does the same with the other hip when I attempt to go that way. It would be humorous if I wasn't so angry and scared and... defeated.

"Don't waste your time. He told me everything."

I think of Helene in the next room, holding Drew's hand, perhaps already sipping the pain from him like broken glass through a straw. I know she, like me, would never make anyone again. This may be a petty, vengeful move on Cillian's part, but I've come to understand his resentment, his jealousy over Helene's presence. This band wasn't enough for me, so why did I expect it would be enough for these guys? It never occurred to me that the boys would see Helene as a threat.

"He told me what you'll do," Conor continues. His eyes scan me, big, glassy, hopeful. "I'm not into girls, but we could do it with a kiss, right? Is that how you turned Cillian?"

I put my hand on his shoulder and he drops his arms. Behind him, Sylvy stirs on the couch, pulling his arm up under his pillow before settling back into a soft, rhythmic snore.

"Okay," I say. "C'mon."

18.

Cillian was right: Conor tastes so, so good.

Pancakes with Dad, Easter baskets, a first kiss with a beautiful boy in a backyard strung with fairy lights. He's warm milk and rabbit fur and boundless energy on my tongue. Cillian may have told him how it works, but Conor stays recklessly open to me, never even squirming in my grip as I take more than I intended. He's not concerned that I give him nothing, that he's emptying himself into me based on an empty promise. He's swollen with hope and the ecstasy of collapse as I pass him to Helene.

Her eyes meet mine over his shoulder. She may be sipping slower than I did, but I can see her filling with his youth, anticipation, that nerve-wracking, exhilarating moment when he introduced himself to Cillian at the bar and bought him a drink. When Helene passes Conor back to me, he's still clinging to the recent memory of Cillian's fingers in his hair as they lounged in his bed. Lips sealed to his, I take that and dig deeper. The screaming, the pile of bodies at the club, a woman falling in the stampede as he rushed Cillian to his car. I take everything from the last twenty-four hours, then a little extra taste of that sweet childhood where he was always wanted, always accepted, always loved.

I'm not going to let you kill him.

Behind me, a gasping breath, followed by the shifting of an uneasy body on sheets soaked in sweat and blood.

I pull away from Conor and turn around. Though clearly still weak, Drew is now propped up on his elbows, his mouth agape. I haven't heard him speak since before the band went on stage, and I can't be sure his mind isn't still in some torpor or coma, but his gaze is pinned to Conor. There is no pain worse than want.

Helene and I walk Conor over to the bed and lower him within Drew's reach. His lips latch onto Conor's slack mouth and right away he eagerly pulls in all the sweetness and comfort I can still taste along the back of my teeth. This won't save Drew, but he'll do what I can't.

A brittle armature of leeched-dry bones and crepe paper skin, the empty husk that used to be Conor, slides onto the floor right as I hear Cillian yell my name.

"You fucking hypocrite."

Cillian is standing in the doorway, features set in hard lines as he shakes his head at me. There's more to it than just anger, though; when his gaze drifts to Conor, he looks sick, stricken. "He was mine."

Helene moves towards him, but I step in front of her.

"This is your fault," I tell Cillian. "We're here—we lost everything—because of you. All those people you killed tonight—they weren't enough for you? You're mad because I ate your snack? You're going to get us all killed. How could you tell him what we are?"

He shoots a piercing glare at Helene. "How could you tell her?"

"It's not the same."

At that, Cillian laughs the kind of bitter, tight-lipped laugh he saves for me alone. Drew, fallen back onto the sheets in a stupor of either pain or overindulgence, groans then folds his arm over his gaping stomach. A trickle of iridescent black liquid oozes from his cleaved tunnel, the last of Conor flooding the sheets.

"It's the same fucking thing, you hypocrite." Cillian draws out the word, barbing every syllable with ire. "You have her, but you won't let me—you won't let the rest of us—have someone of our own. I didn't ask you to make me a succubus, Ronnie. You did what you wanted and we all have to live with that. I think you're pissed that I'm enjoying myself. That I'm fucking *alive*. It's not my fault you won't allow yourself to be who you are. It's not my fault you're ashamed."

"Helene is—"

"Don't say she's different. You don't know how I feel. You don't know what Conor means to me."

"You just met him!"

He flings a hand towards Helene, who is now standing opposite the door, next to the bed. She watches him the same way she did in the diner, impassive yet straightening, filling space. "You just met her!"

"So you love him?" I ask. "You met him, what, five hours ago and you're in love?" I glance at Conor slumped on the floor on the other side of Drew's bed. "I mean, I know love is fleeting, but wow…I can tell you're really crushed."

Cillian pushes past me into the room, bumping my shoulder with his. He kneels on the floor in front of Conor's frail, wizened body and pushes a wave of pale blonde hair—the darker tones leeched from him along with his youth and his strength and whatever talents and memories made him him—from his face. As he traces gentle fingers along Conor's jaw and lower lip, I start to believe that Cillian really did find a connection there, a brightness worth standing still for in another booze-soaked disaster like all the others that have blurred together these last six years.

Maybe I'm the one who can't distinguish love from greed.

"Even if you loved him," I say, "you still betrayed us. You told him things we never tell anyone, no matter what. You put us in danger."

Cillian's eyes are heavy, deep dark hollows cradling bloodshot blue, effortless charm traded for a weariness I have never seen on him. He keeps his gaze on Conor as he speaks. "And you didn't? What did you tell her, Ronnie? What did you promise her? She's not hanging around here because she loves you."

So he doesn't know. Jack never said a word. Still, my chest is tight, adrenaline clawing at my sternum, forcing itself out from between my ribs. I can't look at Helene, not when my mind is clinging to her simple declaration of love in the bathroom, not when I questioned it even in that moment, even though it was what I wanted to hear more than anything.

"I didn't promise her anything," I tell Cillian. My words are as tight as my body, clipped with a cruelty I've been saving up. "I would never promise something I couldn't deliver. You had no right, Cillian. You really think I'd make Conor into one of us, after everything you've put me through? I will never, ever do that again. You're an abomination. You're my mistake."

At that, Cillian springs to his feet and rushes me, slamming me into the wall before I can react. Head spinning, vision blurred, I'm sliding down the cold paint and plaster, and his mouth is over mine as my ass hits the floor. I can't push him off me, and my tunnel can't unclench fast enough to pull from him before he's fully latched onto me. *Up up up*, everything's going in the wrong direction, turning me inside out. My clawing hands drop, arms limp as he sucks out what little energy my muscles have stored. My memory of kissing Rachel in the back of her SUV while Helene worked Caleb up front becomes a gap in my brain as the experience itself is snatched away. Jack passing me a joint, Drew punching a bouncer in Minneapolis, that first butter and steam taste of Helene that night in the alley...*up up up* and devoured by the beast I made. I feel the fissures form in my skin as it tightens and dries. It's happening so fucking fast. Cillian is stripping away every last piece of me and I can't—

I'm flat on my back, but Cillian isn't on top of me anymore. In a blur of black hair and pale skin and an angry red mouth, he's swept off me and onto the floor beside me. His arms and legs flail, fingers clawing at my bare arm, as Helene straddles him. Her face is pressed into his, mouth stretched over his, and I watch his skin go slack and the black cede to grey in his hair as she drains him in front of me.

Jack and Sylvy stand in the doorway, eyes solid black with shock. I want to sit up, explain what happened, but my body is heavy, slow. They both turn, the sound of jumbled footsteps quickening down the hall.

I'm the one who finishes Cillian off. Helene brings him to me like we brought Conor to Drew, and I take what little there is left: an ounce of swagger, the elastic motion of his limbs, a memory of a woman approaching the band in the alley behind a club as they loaded out six years ago. I never knew Cillian remembered that night so well, that he thought I was exciting and beautiful.

Because of that it was easy, making the band into succubi that night in central California six year ago. In their motel room we passed around a bottle, a little molly, laughing and learning about each other and indulging until we were as loose and slippery as newborns seeking warm skin. I wanted to kiss them as much as they wanted to kiss me, as if we all thought we could burrow into each other, become something together that was more than just sex. Jack was the last to fall asleep, so I approached him first, straddling him as Drew snoozed in the bed next to us. He was easy, open, giving in to my hunger even though I could feel his own hunger pushing through his hands on my body. He didn't seem to know what was happening beyond the carnal desire we were fulfilling. He didn't struggle until it was too late, pupils dilated with fear as his muscles unspooled to shuddering inertia beneath me.

Drew was next, stirred by the rocking of the bed. He kept glancing at Jack, who appeared to be simply asleep despite the deep hollows that had formed below his cheeks and around his eyes. Next was Syvly in the next bed, who pulled me to him before I was even done with Drew. Cillian was last, tender and wet-eyed and eager to please. I drank in their sweat, their musk, excited by the power to create new creatures who were entirely mine. All in a row, I left each of them slack, black-eyed rabbits succumbed to the exhaustion of pleasure then fear.

I took their strength, their energy, a random memory or two, a few years from their pasts and their futures. I drained them to the brink of death, but left all of their musical talent and their instinct intact because that was why I followed them, why I wanted them.

Then, as they lay dying, I filled each of them with my mother's scorn and the rabbit fear I could never shake and all the things that made me a succubus before I even knew what that meant. It wasn't poison, but it was a part of me I wanted to share if I couldn't destroy it. I wanted those I made to feel what it was really like to be born a succubus;

if they didn't have their own memories, at least that knowledge would live deep down in their bones.

It was so beautiful, watching them slip then transform under my touch. Terror blooming into revelation. In the morning, they saw a whole new world. They saw who I was, who they now were. A family. I'd never had anyone to share my hunger.

This moment with Cillian now, an echo of draining him to the precipice of rebirth all those years ago, would feel the same as the night I made the band, except what fills my gut—what taints these memories with a film same as the bitterness on my tongue—is grief, the knowledge that this is an ending, not the beginning I had so desperately wanted back then. I had never thought ahead to how this might end. I just *wanted*. Yet here we are. Same as then, I'm so hungry, so out of control, that, even though I know better, I touch my belly as I'm feeding. It's clean, dry, intact.

Even after he's dead, Helene has to pry me off Cillian. Nothing left to take, but I want to hold him. He's small and light in my arms, a pile of hollow bones bound by withered flesh. As Drew's raspy wheezing becomes more sporadic above us, I can't escape that the end is here, as all-at-once as the beginning I forced upon this band those years ago. I hate that my last words to Cillian were "abomination" and "mistake". I'm not sure I ever loved him, but he didn't need to know that.

Helene sits next to me and lifts up his shirt. Cillian's stomach is split from naval to sternum, a thin film of dark, gelatinous goo the only thing holding his intestines inside. Everything he ate tonight shimmers and flows, still alive in a way, lava behind a veil of flesh on the verge of collapse.

19.

They're still here. The van, the money—after witnessing Helene feeding on Cillian, Jack and Sylvy should've taken off with all that we had, left Helene and me to sort out our survival with a dying Drew and two more bodies we can't hide. They shouldn't be sitting on the couch in the living room, waiting for me.

"Were you ever gonna tell us?" Sylvy asks. He's stacks of wavering lines, even the smallest movements building towards either springing up and out the door or right into me.

Jack won't even look at me.

"He was sick," I say. "Almost as bad as Drew."

Sylvy's eyes narrow. "So you let your girlfriend have him? Your girlfriend who's a fucking succubus too?"

"He attacked me. He was out of control."

"Aren't we too, though? Look at where we are now." Sylvy throws up his hands. "You gonna let her kill us too, or are you gonna do it yourself?"

"We are mistakes, after all," Jack adds.

Mistakes. That word in Jack's mouth, used to hurt me the same why I used it to hurt Cillian. Nothing will lessen the heavy truth of that, the seed planted in my mind even as I sat in that motel room with the band six years ago.

"He was suffering," I say, "like Drew's suffering."

Sylvy rises from the couch. "So you had your girlfriend put him down? Am I—is Jack next? Is that all we are to you, rabid dogs?"

Jack stands too, stepping in front of Sylvy. "C'mon. We don't need to—"

"Really?" He pushes Jack aside, continuing to glower over me as he speaks. "Don't you get it, man? She's never going to love you. But me, you and me…Where's your loyalty? We've known each other since we were twenty years old."

"Sylvy, you're sick," I say. It comes out softer, sadder than I intended.

"I'm fucking fine!"

I grab the hem of his shirt and lift it up. His torso is wrapped several times over in torn bedsheets, black rot bloomed like watercolor bursts all over his stomach. Jack suppresses a gag as the acrid odor fills the space between us.

"What Helene did to Cillian she could've done to you in the club last night," I tell Sylvy. "I know you needed me, but you took too much. You were out of control and you tried to drain me. That's what this is. You will eat and eat and kill everyone in your path and it will never satisfy you. You'll get sicker and sicker and you'll die alone in the van or a motel room, or in a jail cell. It's getting worse for all of us and we can't fix this."

"What about you?" Sylvy snatches the hem of my shirt, but I'm able to push him away. "When it's your time, is your girlfriend gonna put you down too?"

Everything in me wants to say yes. I wish I could show him a cleaved and disintegrating tunnel spilling from my guts. I want to tell him how I've had a hunger I've never been able to satisfy since I was born, tell the two I have left—the succubi I made—that I will gladly kneel at Helene's feet and allow her to drain me, all the while crying tears of relief as she delivers me into oblivion. I want to hurt the way Sylvy hurts.

"It won't happen to me," I say. "Helene's been through this before with someone she made. It doesn't happen to those who are born a succubus. It only happens to those we make because—"

"We're an abomination," Jack finishes.

"I didn't mean that," I say.

"It's true, though. We weren't supposed to exist and now we…won't."

Sylvy looks to Jack before turning back to me. He seems smaller now, hunched, hands nervously crossing back and forth over his stomach. "You're afraid of me? You think I'm some wild animal you'll have to kill before I kill you?"

"You can't help it, Sylvy."

Down the hall, there's the soft click of a door opening. We all turn to see Helene standing outside Drew's room. She looks both shaken and numb at the same time.

"He's gone," she says.

Jack looks at me. "Drew."

"You fucking killed him!" Sylvy screams.

He's electric lines sizzling, any weakness smothered by one last burst of energy, though I can't tell which way he's going to charge. My first thought is that he'll barrel through me and go after Helene, and I've already braced myself to stop him in any way I can, including draining him dead right here in front of Jack. But then, just as Sylvy pitches forward, Helene doubles over and, with a hand braced against the wall, proceeds to vomit a rush of black bile onto the hardwood floor. The front door slams. When I turn around, it's only Jack and I in the living room.

20.

Because Sylvy has nowhere to go and no way to get there—the keys to the van are in Jack's pocket—Jack thinks he's too weak to go very far and will come back to us soon. "He just needs some air," he says. When he makes a wry comment about how any one of them would prefer to die in a comfortable bed instead of alone on the sidewalk, my stomach clenches.

Really, the pain—the hunger—will become unbearable, and when that happens Sylvy will drain some poor soul on a predawn dog-walk, or he'll break into a neighbor's house and slaughter the family inside. Like with Cillian, that breaking point will come swiftly and unexpectedly. Though Helene is still nauseous, she insists on going after him and I let her.

It gives Jack some time to say goodbye to his brothers.

Drew doesn't look like Cillian. Though he's frail and small, papery skin sucked tight against a network of disjointed bones, he still looks like himself. He looks like he quietly slipped away in a hospital bed while Jack and I were getting coffee. His limbs are crossed under the quilt, thin blue veins bright on his closed eyelids. Only the oily black liquid smeared around his mouth remains proof of the disease that ate him alive.

So Helene did it. She sucked out his pain, poisoned herself so he could drift away peacefully instead of writhing in unrelenting hunger.

She did what I was supposed to do.

Jack is silent. He spends a long time at Drew's bedside, watching him, then kneels in front of Cillian's body on the floor and does the same. His movements are stiff, rickety from exhaustion or long car rides or age—I don't know. *I can t see myself standing on a stage in some shithole when I m sixty-five*, he said to me less than twenty-four hours ago. *I m tired, Ronnie, and I know you re tired too.*

"You have it, don't you?" I say. I've known since the green room, when I saw that small dark crescent in his naval. Even with everything going on, I can't shake what I saw. I can't lie to myself anymore. "You've been scared for awhile."

Jack nods. His eyes drift to Conor on the other side of Drew's bed, but he doesn't ask. I want to tell him how Cillian betrayed us, but there's no point. Maybe it's better he doesn't know that part.

"I'm sorry, Jack. I'm sorry about everything."

When he finally looks up at me, his hazel eyes are bright, almost mischievous. It's every late night of just me and him, leaned up against the van, passing a joint back and forth while the others sleep. "So, what do you think of this place?"

I laugh. I can't help myself. It feels good.

"Seriously," he says. "I think I've got some time, and I'd like to settle down. I want to live in a nice little house in a nice little town and die in my own bed."

God, do I want that for him too.

I gesture at the room around us. "Well, it looks like you'll get your wish."

After we laugh, Jack's expression turns dark and serious again. I lower myself in front of him, so that we're both kneeling before Cillian's withered body. I imagine Helene in a bush down the block, draining the last drops of life out of Sylvy. When the sun comes up, a resident will find his corpse and call the police. Within hours, the police will knock on this door and find three more desiccated bodies inside. Jack will never get to peacefully slip away in a cozy bed surrounded by the safety of four walls that are his. I will never be able to give Jack the kind of comfort he deserves because we have no home, no beacon to call us back to who we were before this. I'm forever a guest, whether it's in a motel room or my own life.

"What I said...I didn't mean it," I tell him. "My mistake was that I didn't give you a choice. I'm sorry for what I did to you—what I did to all of you. That was so fucking selfish of me. I had no right."

He squeezes my upper arm, letting his fingers trail down over the back of my hand. "No, you were right, Ronnie. This is nature correcting itself." He offers me a gentle smile, and it hurts more than anything else tonight. "So, how long do you think we've got this nice little house in this nice little town?"

I draw my arm around Jack's shoulders and pull him into me. He loosens in my embrace, tucks his face into my neck, and exhales. I'm glad he can't see me cry.

21.

This is how it goes:

In a little yellow house in a little town in Idaho, a merch girl holds a guitarist in her arms and kisses him for a long, long time. There are no promoters and bouncers, no gin and tonics, no condescending *sweethearts* and *ma'ams*. The guitarist kisses back, opening himself all the way up to her. It's a mercy, an escape, the easiest ending. The guitarist trusts her to give this to him. This is how he wants to go.

It's not easy for the merch girl. For me.

I can't bear the thought of him shrinking in my embrace. He's supposed to drift off gently, his mind emptying of every worry, every fear, as his bones hollow and his muscles atrophy and his skin dries and cracks. He won't have to face the pain of his body turning on him, the decision I made six years ago finally catching up and tearing him apart while I wipe my chin and sigh my regrets.

He's supposed to be the fourth body in the house, a picture on the news, while Helene and I spend the rest of our days looking over our shoulders, checking fan sites and message boards for our names and photos. I'll carry that, but the hardest part will be doing this one last thing for the person who is as close to a best friend as I've ever had.

So, sitting on the floor, surrounded by those I made and destroyed, I hold Jack in my lap and sip slowly. I work my way backwards. First, I take the fresh memory of seeing Helene drain Cillian in this room. Jack drifts quickly, eyes closed, so he does not have to see and fear these bodies as the memories loosen from him. Next, selfishly, I take my horrible words—"abomination" and "mistake"—from his mind. I take last night, the band's performance, the pile of bodies in the hall behind the stage, everyone Jack drained, that horrible feeling of being unable to pry himself from those poor people even as he watched them wither and collapse in his own embrace. The guilt, the tunnel-vision fear when he felt that first cramp in his stomach after he saw Drew's own cleaved and rotting tunnel—I take it all. I take the kiss I blew to him outside the motel as Helene ushered me inside. I take Spokane, all of Washington, Helene. I take pieces of his memories from all the years we've known each other, just enough that he won't remember my name, or my face, or the things I've said to him. I will just be a vague memory of some merch girl who spent one tour with them, selling t-shirts and keeping to herself, doing it for the love of the band.

I should take his strength, the skill in his hands, the muscle memory of chords and stretching fingers and that rush of his body moving faster than his mind under stage lights. I should drink all the way down to the first time he picked up a guitar, his mother sitting at the piano with him, the smell of his father's aftershave. I owe him the gentleness of oblivion.

Instead, what I do next is futile. I suck *up up up* all the rot that has been slowly forming in his gut. I empty his deteriorating tunnel, not healing it but merely stilling the disease's progression for now. This will only prolong his suffering, I know, but right now and maybe for the next few weeks or months, he'll find peace in the gaps between these miseries.

It's a drunken daze I've left him in, that moment when your last thought, as you're drifting off to sleep, is how bad the hangover is going to be. I slide Jack off my lap, grab a pillow from the bed and arrange it under his head. Outside,

I vomit black bile onto the driveway before grabbing what I need from the van and Helene's car.

Back in the house, I take a moment to look at Jack for the last time. He looks like any other night, curled away from Drew or Sylvy in the motel bed next to mine, a still moment between restless dreams and endless roads. I feel ashamed that I don't have any tears. I've been weak, but, in this moment, I think I did the right thing. He'll be free now, same as me.

In the living room, a door opens. The frantic, familiar clip of Helene's boots stopped short on their way to me. Then a heave, and the splatter of what I know is black bile—the last of Sylvy—hitting the hardwood floor.

I tuck the $800 cash we made in Spokane into Jack's jeans. I slip the key to Helene's car into his resting palm.

Six weeks later and the back of the van still smells of Cillian's pomade, a heavy vanilla that used to make me carsick on early mornings. Strands of Sylvy's long black hair jut from the seats' seams. A watery black stain, the size of a silver dollar, mars the back bench where Drew last laid.

Up front is better. It's mostly Helene up there now, the scents of juniper and pepper and burnt almonds warming the space, making a familiar home. Sometimes I catch a whiff of myself: the mineral meatiness of my scalp, a dirty penny smell on my fingers, the lingering burp of a fast food burger eaten too fast. Jack remains in the occasional breath of weed, the worn spots on the steering wheel, the muscle memory of a seat molded to his shape.

While Helene drives, I sit in the back with one of Jack's guitars, clumsily strumming along to online videos. Though she gave me everything she took—the movement of Drew's fingers on his bass, Sylvy whirring against the drums, Cillian's showman strut—I keep it all stored away as a memory. Maybe I'll need to draw from those gifts one day, maybe I won't. Helene's the singer, not me.

We'll stand together on a stage, working our way through every dive bar in every town that will have us. Montana gets the worst of me, with my stumbling fingers, but I'm hoping I'll be able to play the guitar with confidence by the time we get to Michigan. I'm enjoying catching eyes, having choices, being the focus of even one person's ravenous attention instead of the other way around. It feels as right as standing behind a merch table.

As good as it feels, though, the road doesn't cure hunger, no more than a stage or a motel room or even a new love. We'll always be hungry, me and Helene, because that is who we are. And maybe I don't want to always sleep alone.

Acknowledgements

Though it took almost two years from start to finish, this is the story that poured out of me like nothing else I've ever written. Ronnie's been knocking around in my head for a long time, but it took even longer for me to realize that people might want to read about a woman—feeling her age, feeling her worth shrinking, feeling all her loneliness and resentment and mistakes—and a band existing in that wide, unacknowledged space between being Nobodies and Somebodies. All the thanks to the people in my life who convinced me that it was time to let Ronnie out.

That said, it takes many hands to make a book. Whether it was reading early drafts, providing advice, sharing knowledge, or being a source of support throughout this journey, much gratitude to these lovely people:

Matt McCarthy

Emily Verona

Scott Moses

Hailey Piper

My fellow Nervous Drivers (AD, AL, AS, CN, SA, SL, TB)

A heap of thanks to Waylon Jordan and Off Limits Press for their hard work and giving this book a comfortable home away from the road.

Much thanks to Evangeline Gallagher for creating Ronnie and Helene on this gorgeous cover.

My gratitude and admiration to the talented authors who blurbed this book.

And my thanks to you, readers, for taking a chance on this queer little succubi story.

Author Bio

J.A.W. McCarthy is the Shirley Jackson Award nominated author of Sometimes We're Cruel and Other Stories (Cemetery Gates Media, 2021) and Sleep Alone (Off Limits Press, 2023). Her short fiction has appeared in numerous publications, including *Vastarien*, *PseudoPod*, *LampLight*, *Apparition Lit*, *Tales to Terrify*, and *The Best Horror of the Year Vol 13* (ed. Ellen Datlow). She is Thai American and lives with her husband and assistant cats in the Pacific Northwest. You can call her Jen on Twitter @JAWMcCarthy and find out more at www.jawmccarthy.com.